FIRE & LIGHT

BOOK ONE

DRAGONFIRE SAGA

LOVELIGHT

FIRE & LIGHT

First Edition: Dec 2025

ISBN 979-8-9941109-0-4 (Hardcover)
ISBN 979-8-9941109-1-1 (Paperback)
ISBN 979-8-9941109-2-8 (ebook)

Cover design and Editing by
Lovelight Productions

Published by Lovelight Productions
Wichita Falls, Texas
www.lovelight-books.com

For everyone who ever felt like the storm inside them was too big to hold.

For my brother and sister, who will forever soar in my dreams, the first dragons to be set free.

"*I am made of memories and rage, and a handful of bones. I am not as soft as the storms that gather in my lungs.*"

——Nikita Gill

THE PROPHECY

When earth grows still and sky weeps ash,
when fire meets storm in children's clasp,
six marks shall wake the sleeping chain,
and love long lost shall rise again.

Four for flame, for wind, for stone, for sea,
one for the child, and one for the plea.
When their hearts align and mercy bends,
the curse will break, or the world will end.

CHAPTER 1

ALLIE

*L*ena's voice cracked like a fault line. The message had been waiting for three hours. Allie did not want to hear it. But she pressed play anyway.

"Allie, I need your help. Something's wrong with a supplier. I don't trust what they're asking. Please come tonight. I'll explain when you get here."

Then silence. Too tight. Too still.

Allie Grayson was four years and a lifetime past law school. She was twenty-nine, but with eyes that had seen too much. Too young for the grief she carried, too old in the way she looked at the world. She wore her blazer like armor and kept her hair pulled tight, as if order could protect her from everything that did not make sense. Storm-blue eyes scanned the room.

She was sturdy and no-nonsense, a brunette like their father, with Texas still in her stride. Mara had been the golden one, with blonde hair, blue eyes, and a laugh that could derail a train. Allie had learned to be the steady one. The smart one. The one who stayed behind and picked up the pieces.

The pendant at her throat pressed cold against her skin. Dull

3

silver, blue stone, heavy with memory. She touched it without thinking, ignoring the faint itch it always left behind. It had belonged to Mara. The discomfort was a small price for keeping her close.

The case file on her desk remained open. Her first real courtroom case. A clean fraud investigation. Cut and dry. Judge Raines at ten a.m. tomorrow morning. She was a junior ADA in the fraud division. Spreadsheets, subpoenas, paper trails. Clean work. Logical.

She should have been excited, but tomorrow also marked three years since her sister's death, and tonight Lena's voicemail had carved straight through that tidy life like a scalpel.

The grief did not hit like it used to. It pressed quieter now. Deeper. The official report said an accident. No foul play. Case closed. But the guardrail had been scorched, and no one ever explained why. Allie had never stopped asking. She had just learned to ask smarter.

She tucked documents into her briefcase. She buttoned her coat, locked her office, and left behind corridors of files and fluorescent light.

A yellow cab rolled to a stop at the curb. Headlights swept over wet pavement. A fine mist hung in the air, not quite rain but enough to dampen surfaces. It smelled faintly of concrete, ozone, and car exhaust. Her own car was still at Lena's bar. She had left it behind after drinks last night.

"The Black Cat," Allie said. She slid into the back seat.

Dallas blurred past the glass. Neon signs blinked overhead. Colors bled into slick pavement. Streetlights strobed across the windshield in rhythmic bursts. By the time the cab turned into Deep Ellum, music had already reached her, spilled from bar doors and narrow alleys. Laughter drifted from patios crowded despite the cold.

The cab pulled to the curb. Allie paid quickly and stepped out. October air cut through her blazer. Her briefcase hung at her side, heavier now. She looked up at the flickering sign of The Black Cat.

She paused in the doorway and let her eyes adjust to the dim light before stepping inside. Her heels clicked softly against the scuffed tile as she took in the noise, the haze, and the layered scent of The Black

Cat. The bar was half full. A saxophone's last note faded into the murmur of voices.

"Allie." Lena stood behind the bar in boots and jeans, auburn hair pulled back in a messy twist. A worried edge tugged at her smile.

Allie had not realized how much she needed to be seen.

Lena's grin spread wide as she leaned across the counter and pulled her into a quick hug. "Look at you, counsellor. Navy blazer. Heels. I rarely get the full getup in here. Almost didn't recognize you."

Allie smiled. "Big hearing tomorrow. Figured I'd practice looking important."

Lena laughed and slid a glass across the bar. "Of course you did. And for the record? You look hot. What's your poison tonight, counsellor? Water or something with teeth?"

"Water," Allie said, the word falling heavier than she liked. "Need a clear head."

She took the glass, then studied Lena's face. Beneath the grin, her eyes looked tired. Cheeks flushed. Jaw tight.

"You sounded upset in your message. What's going on?"

Lena's hands stilled on the glass she was drying. She set it down carefully. Too carefully. Her eyes flicked toward the door, then back. As if making sure they were still alone.

"Lena." Allie's voice dropped. "What's wrong?"

They had promised not to talk about Mara's death on the anniversary. The first year, they had spent the day together, but it had left them hollow. It had left them sadder than before. They had agreed to give it time. They had agreed to grieve apart until they could remember Mara without breaking open. Now, one day from that date, the call felt wrong. It was too close. It was too heavy. And Allie could not shake the feeling that Lena was holding something back.

Lena's hand brushed the towel in her palm. The knot was dark with rust-colored blood.

"What happened to your hand?"

"Just a knife slip," she said quickly. "Nothing."

The stain looked too deep. Too dark. And Lena would not meet her eyes.

"If it's just supplier trouble, why call me at all?" Allie asked.

Lena tried to laugh, but the sound cracked. "There's something…" Her voice thinned. Her eyes pulled toward the door like a reflex, then snapped back. "About Mara. Something I should've told you sooner." Her fingers twisted the towel tight enough to make the blood seep faster.

Allie's stomach tightened. The glass felt slick in her hand. The pendant burned cold at her throat, tighter than usual, as if it sensed the shift in the air. She resisted the urge to pull it away from her skin.

"What do you mean?"

Lena looked down at her hand. The towel was already seeping through. "You have to promise me you'll keep an open mind."

"That's not a great way to start a conversation."

"I mean it."

Allie nodded slowly. "Okay."

"Not here," Lena whispered. "Let me close up first. We'll talk in the office."

Unease prickled at Allie's neck. One by one, Lena ushered the last patrons out. The jukebox clicked silent. The bartender slipped away through the side door. The Black Cat settled into its closing rhythm. Glasses stacked. Clean, sharper in the air. A tired jazz record spun behind the bar.

Allie stayed on her stool, her glass untouched. She watched the towel around Lena's hand darken as minutes stretched. The air thickened with everything Lena would not say.

"I'm going to use the restroom," Allie said. "Then we'll talk."

"Sure." Lena managed a smile that did not reach her eyes. "I'll just take the trash out. Be right back."

Allie slipped down the hallway, past the prep counter and stacked crates. The bathroom door clicked shut behind her. She leaned against the sink and stared at her reflection. Dark circles under her eyes. Hair pulled so tight it looked painful. The pendant caught the light, cold and heavy against her throat.

Three years.

She turned on the tap. Cold water rushed over her hands.
Then the scream tore through the walls.

"Allie!"

Raw. Desperate. Unmistakable.

Allie ran.

CHAPTER 2

LENA

The moment the door closed behind Allie, Lena's smile fell. She stared at her hand. Blood had soaked through the towel. The cut pulsed with each heartbeat, but that was not what made her fingers shake.

It was the voice. The one she had heard three years ago in the rain. The one who had just ordered whiskey at her bar.

Earlier that afternoon, the bar had been quiet. Two regulars nursed drinks. She had moved on autopilot, wiping down the counter, but her mind kept circling back to the pendant. It had warmed against her skin. Just a pulse.

She told herself it was nothing, but the feeling lingered under her ribs. When one of the patrons laughed too hard at his own joke, his elbow swept wide and knocked a half-full glass toward the edge of the counter.

Lena reacted without thinking. A breath of pressure left her palm. Subtle. Almost nothing.

The water inside the glass froze mid-slosh. Stillness. Dense. Time did not stop. Just the water. That was enough.

The sudden weight shift steadied the glass long enough for her to catch it. The man did not notice. Neither did the one beside him. But Lena did.

She turned away quickly, grabbing a rag to hide the flush rising in her cheeks. "Brilliant," she muttered. "Distracted by your own dragon."

She pressed her hand to the pendant. The metal felt cooler now, but the pulse still lingered beneath her skin. She had promised her father control. Sworn she would not repeat the mistakes that had already stained the Kors bloodline.

The Alliance did not need another reason to question it. In her distraction, she failed to notice the door had opened. Failed to see the figure near the entrance.

She looked up too late. A hooded man stood in the corner where the light did not quite reach. Silent. Still. Watching. He had been there the whole time. He had seen everything.

Her stomach dropped. The rag slipped from her hands. When he finally spoke, his voice came low and rough.

"Whiskey. Neat."

The last time she had heard that voice had been three years ago. The call from Mara had come frantic, begging for help. Lena reached Highway 10 and spotted the wreck from a quarter mile out. Mara's car was crashed into the guardrail.

She stopped with the engine idling, heart pounding. Two men moved through the scene with military precision. One swept a flashlight across the wreckage. They were gone before the police arrived.

One of them had spoken. Calm. Cold. "The Alliance will handle it. Clean the mess before anyone notices."

She had stayed hidden. Headlights off. Hands frozen on the wheel. She never told the police. Never told Allie.

The Alliance kept the world blind to dragons. Which meant something had gone horribly wrong with Mara. Now, the same chill curled up her spine.

Her hand shook as she poured, but she managed to set the glass in front of him without spilling. He lifted it, took a slow sip, and his eyes never left hers.

"Careful," he said. "Wouldn't want another accident. Like the one on Highway 10."

The air left Lena's lungs. He smelled wrong. Beneath the cologne was ozone and burnt copper. The scar near his eye caught the light, pale against his skin.

He knew about Mara. He knew about Highway 10. And he knew about Allie.

He finished the whiskey in one swallow. Set the glass down. Dropped a twenty on the bar. As he turned, something slipped from his coat pocket.

A matchbook. Black paper. Silver lettering. *Dragon's Breath.*

He did not notice. The door swung shut behind him. Lena stood frozen. Her hands shook so badly she could barely grip the bar.

She turned to steady herself and reached for the cutting board. The paring knife was still there. She needed to do something. Anything. Keep her hands busy.

She grabbed a lemon. The knife slipped. It bit deep across her palm. She hissed and grabbed a bar towel, wrapping it tight. Blood soaked through instantly.

Her eyes drifted back to the matchbook. Her father had played with that band once, before the burnout. Before the Alliance stepped in.

She picked it up with shaking hands. Inside, someone had drawn a symbol. The same one etched into Mara's pendant clasp.

Whoever killed Mara knew about Allie now. Lena could not stay silent anymore.

Her fingers rose to the pendant she wore. The twin to Allie's. She traced the edges. It had never meant anything before. Until now.

She pulled a pen from the register and wrote inside the matchbook cover, then slipped it into her apron pocket. Three years of silence. She had almost let it become four.

They had promised not to talk about Mara on the anniversaries, but some things could no longer be left unspoken. She dialed. When voicemail answered, her voice cracked.

"Allie, I need your help. Something's wrong with a supplier. I don't trust what they're asking. Please come by tonight. I'll explain when you get here."

Supplier trouble. Safe words wrapped around panic. If anyone else heard it, they would hear nothing unusual. But Allie would know.

By the time Allie walked in, Lena's smile was stitched back in place. The lie rehearsed. The fear buried deep.

She only needed to hold it together a little longer. Just long enough to tell the truth. Then she finished closing. The last light clicked off.

Allie had excused herself to the restroom. Lena grabbed the trash bags from behind the bar. Cold mist touched her face as she stepped into the alley.

The bags were heavy in her hands. A figure stepped from the shadows. Black coat. Pale hands. Eyes that caught the light wrong. Blade glinting.

The trash bags fell. "Who sent you?" she snapped.

She grabbed a bottle from a crate. Glass slick with condensation. Her father's voice whispered through memory. *Fight like the tide. Flow and strike.*

The man moved. His knife came fast, aimed low. She twisted and swung the bottle hard into his forearm.

Glass exploded. His grunt came sharp and pained. Blood welled dark through his sleeve. But he did not drop the knife.

He lunged again. The blade caught her across the belly. Not deep, but hot. A line of fire that stole her breath.

She drove her knee up. Felt it connect. He folded forward, wheezing. Her hand moved on instinct. She grabbed at him. Cloth, skin—anything.

Came away with a torn strip of his coat. Black fabric. Wet with his blood.

He snarled. Surged upright. The knife rose. This time it struck high, just below her collarbone.

The world tilted. Sharp. Cold. Then burning.

Her pendant flared hot against her skin. The silver chain began to glow. Red. Then white. Then black. The metal hissed.

The chain snapped. The pendant hit the concrete with a soft clink.

The moment it left her skin, something shifted. The air changed. Her power stirred.

But it was too late. Blood spilled fast and hot down her chest. Her knees buckled. The wall caught her as she slid down.

He did not look at her anymore. One hand pressed to his ribs. The other held the knife. He dragged it across the brick wall in deliberate strokes.

A sigil took shape. Crooked lines. Sharp angles. Wrong geometry. Then he dipped his fingers into the blood pooling at her side.

She tried to move. Could not. He smeared her blood across the carved lines. Once. Twice. Nothing.

Then the blood began to glow. Faint red, like embers under ash. It pulsed once. Twice. Then faded to rust-brown.

The man straightened. Checked his work. Wiped the knife on his coat and walked away. His footsteps faded into the dark.

Lena's breath rattled. Cold crept into her chest. Heavy and final. This was it.

She had promised to tell Allie the truth. About Mara. About the pendant. About everything.

She had waited three years too long. Her fingers reached for the fallen pendant and closed around it. The metal was still warm.

She gathered what breath she had left. "Allie!"

The scream tore from her throat. Ragged and desperate. It echoed off brick and metal.

Far off, a siren wailed. Tires hissed on wet pavement. A saxophone cried somewhere down the block. Low and mournful.

Alive in the dark. The city kept breathing. Indifferent. Unaware that something ancient had just woken.

Lena's eyes began to close. She had not saved Mara. She would not save Allie.

But maybe the pendant still could.

CHAPTER 3

ALLIE

*A*llie burst from the bathroom and sprinted down the hallway. Her heels skidded on tile. She shouldered through the back door into the alley.

The air reeked of iron and smoke, sharp enough to sting her throat. Lena was crumpled against a stack of boxes. Blood soaked her blouse. Her pendant, clutched in her hand, caught the neon light. Her eyes found Allie's, wide and desperate.

"No, no, no." Allie dropped to her knees. Her palms slipped against the wet ground as she pressed hard on the wound. Hot crimson seeped between her fingers. Too much. Too fast.

"Stay with me. Please."

"Key," Lena rasped. Her voice sounded torn, more air than sound.

With the last of her strength, Lena pushed the pendant into Allie's palm. Her fingers trembled as they closed around hers. The moment their skin touched, the pendant flared. Blue light shot through Allie's fingers, hot and bright. It raced up her arm like lightning through a wire. Her hand locked in place. The sensation was electric and freezing at once, as if the metal had fused to her skin. Allie gasped. She could not pull away. The connection held her until Lena's grip loosened and her hand fell away.

The chain was slick against her palm, warmer than expected. The heat pulsed beneath her skin, as though something had been planted there. Then something deep inside her chest stirred. A pulse that was not her own. It tugged her backwards. Smoke. Shattering glass. A seven-year-old's scream.

Her pendant seared against her collar. Light flared. Silver burst into deep blue. The two pendants pulsed together in rhythm, thrumming through her bones. Sparks crawled along her arms, lifting strands of hair that shimmered faintly. Thunder rolled inside her chest, resonating through muscle and marrow. Her breath caught. Her entire body trembled. She could not move. Fear pinned her in place. Beneath the terror was something else. Recognition. The storm inside her had already begun to answer.

Above them, crimson lines writhed across the brick. At first, they looked like blood, but the curves bent into something deliberate. Fernlike and jagged. Glowing as if alive. The mark pulsed in time with the pendants.

Allie froze.

The sight blurred into memory. A scorched guardrail. Mara's SUV twisted against it. On its side, dim but burned deep, she had seen the same mark. The same pattern. Her stomach lurched. No. This could not be real. The glow faltered, vanished. The rune sagged into streaks of blood. Dull. Ordinary again.

At the mouth of the alley, something moved. A figure, tall and faceless, lingered in the neon wash. Its shape rippled like mist. Edges blurred into shadow. Allie's voice caught in her throat. She tried to scream, but the sound broke. Strangled by fear. The shadow dissolved. Only the rhythm of footsteps remained, fading into the night.

Lena's chest rose once. A shallow, trembling motion. Then it fell still.

When Allie looked back down, Lena's eyes had gone glassy.

"No. No. No." Her voice cracked.

Not again. Not like this.

Allie pressed harder, though her hands slid in blood gone cool.

"Stay with me," she whispered. "Please, stay with me."

The silence that followed was absolute. Her phone nearly slipped from her grip as she forced herself to dial. Her voice cracked when the dispatcher answered. She managed only fragments.

"My friend... she's... she's dying."

Time fractured. Every second dragged. Her heartbeat filled her ears, pounding in sync with the fading warmth from the pendant in her hand. Sirens rose in the distance. Faint at first, then deafening.

Red and blue lights strobed across the alley walls, splitting Lena's face into flashes of color. Painting the blood in cold crimson and blue. Uniformed figures flooded the space. Radios crackled. Boots struck concrete. Someone shouted for medical. Another voice called for perimeter control.

Hands reached for her. Gentle at first, then insistent. Allie twisted away. She clutched Lena's arm and the pendant slick with blood.

"I'm not leaving her," she gasped.

Her own pendant blazed hotter against her chest. Pain lanced through her ribs. Mara's voice rose from memory. Calm and certain.

Feel the storm, Allie.

A flashlight beam sliced across the wall. The bloody lines glimmered and shifted, visible for a single heartbeat before the light moved on. Allie's breath caught. She thought she heard someone whisper the word *Alliance*, though no one nearby spoke. When she looked up, the officers' faces were blank. Routine already smoothing over the impossible.

An officer crouched beside her. His tone was soft.

"Miss, you need to let go."

The paramedics had covered Lena with a sheet. Allie could still see the outline of her hand beneath it. She wanted to pull the sheet back. Needed to ask the questions Lena had promised to answer. Allie had not been the one with secrets.

"Miss Grayson." The officer touched her elbow again.

"Let us get you somewhere warm."

She shook her head.

"I need to stay."

"There is nothing more you can do here."

Nothing more. The words landed like a sentence.

Something in her cracked. Not loud. Not sharp. Quiet, like glass settling after a fall. And three years learning to find truth in buried words. Here, with Lena's blood on her hands, none of it meant anything.

She turned toward the wall. The sigil had stopped glowing. It had become streaks of red that could have been anything. Her mind scrambled for logic, already rewriting what she had witnessed. Blood spatter. Reflection. Shock is playing tricks.

But she had felt the heat. She had seen it pulse with the pendant.

"I saw it," she whispered.

The officer frowned.

"Saw what, counsellor?"

Her throat closed. How could she explain? That the mark had lived. That something had answered it. That reality itself had bent.

"Nothing," she said at last. "I saw nothing."

The lie tasted like copper. Lena's pendant was sealed in her palm, refusing to be pried away. The alley swelled with sound. Radios. Voices. The scent of exhaust and iron.

Behind it all, Allie's heart thundered. The sigil burned behind her eyes. The second she had seen. One on the guardrail where Mara died. One here, carved in brick and blood. Even when she blinked, it remained. Etched into memory like lightning on glass.

She did not know what it meant. Only that whatever had started with her sister was not finished. And as the sirens faded, a single thought took root.

She might be next.

CHAPTER 4

KILLER

*B*y the time the knife had been pulled from her body, the alley had fallen silent. Distant sirens split the night. Laughter drifted from Elm Street, blurred by walls and distance.

They knelt beside the wall. The serpent-hilted knife rested steady in their gloved hand, its weight familiar and cold. The tip dragged through the pooling blood with slow precision. Each stroke curved into the shape whispered by the curse. Lines formed patterns older than memory.

The sigil took form. A circle split by a jagged line, fernlike curls unfurling from its edges. It glowed faint crimson beneath the flickering neon, throbbing like something alive.

The scent of ozone thickened around them. Pain lingered in their ribs where she had struck. A bruise swelled beneath the sleeve. The cut along their forearm ached, weeping. Their blood mixed with hers, feeding the shape carved into the concrete.

Pain was offering. Offering became power. Power became permanence. They exhaled slowly. The alley reeked of copper, grease, and burnt neon. Fluorescent light blinked overhead. Steam rose from a nearby grate.

The pendant lay in her hand. It had snapped from its chain. They left it. Trophies meant nothing. The mark mattered.

Four sigils burned behind their eyes. Each one a death. Each one a measured stroke in a design only they understood.

Crimson faded into stone.

The sigil pulsed once more, feeding them a final surge of strength before falling dormant.

The voice returned. Low. Insistent. Vibrating in the marrow.

Completion was close. Something ancient shifted just beyond perception, waiting for the final mark.

The woman on the ground wheezed. A thin, rattling breath. Her fingers scrabbled weakly across the concrete, reaching for the pendant near the gutter.

She should not still be conscious.

They watched as she closed trembling fingers around the metal.

Then the scream tore loose.

"Allie!"

Raw. Desperate. A dying promise thrown into the dark. The sound ricocheted off brick and metal, carrying straight toward the alley's back entrance.

They froze.

Footsteps.

Light. Quick. Running.

Not from the street.

From the back corridor.

From inside the bar.

They slipped deeper into the shadows, silent as breath.

The door at the alley's end burst open. Neon light splashed across wet pavement. A woman appeared in the glow, hair catching the red wash, eyes wide as she took in the scene.

Recognition hit like a thrown blade. The sister. Storm-born. Unawakened.

She was not supposed to be here.

The sigil at their feet trembled. Its glow faltered, edges pulling out of pattern. The offering was incomplete. The sequence was broken.

They hissed through their teeth. The design was ruined. The offering undone. She had broken the pattern.

Sirens were closer now. Tires hissed across wet pavement. Voices crackled from open radios, sharp with urgency. Their gaze flicked to the sigil. The shape throbbed weakly, light guttering. The mark was wounded. So was the plan.

They stepped into shadow. Boots whispered against concrete. They left no trace. The mark burned behind their eyelids. A command curled through their veins. Pulled them forward.

They exhaled once.

"We're not finished," they said.

Then they vanished. The alley swallowed their shape. Neon flickered above the blood-soaked ground. Smoke curled from a nearby vent, carrying the scent of something burning. Somewhere on Elm Street, a saxophone bent a lonely note. The voice inside them bent with it.

CHAPTER 5

ERIK

$\mathscr{E}$rik Varg's black truck rumbled through the streets of Dallas. The dashboard clock showed 11:52 p.m., Thursday night, less than thirty minutes since Torvald's call.

Torvald's voice had come through clipped and professional. A murder at the Black Cat Lounge. Victim Lena Kors. Possible witness. Sigil at the scene. Torvald did not call unless it mattered. The Alliance's liaison in Dallas kept things tight. Facts, not theories. Never more than needed. Tonight he had needed Erik.

The skyline shimmered in glass and neon, but beneath the modern glow he felt something older pressing against the night. The fire woven through his blood stirred whenever dragon violence touched the city. Tonight it burned like coal beneath his skin, a warning older than any signal crackling through the radio mounted to his dash.

William Kors had once played drums for Dragon's Breath before the Alliance placed him under protection. He was water-touched and unstable. His power had manifested in tides that could drown him as easily as anyone else. If the victim was his daughter, something larger was in motion.

He turned onto Elm Street. Police lights flared at the alley entrance. Red and blue flooded across wet brick in rhythmic pulses.

Officers moved with practiced rhythm, stringing tape between rusted dumpsters and calling out clipped orders over the hum of generators. The air carried the familiar tang of copper, layered with ozone and a faint trace of ash.

Not fire like his, but water. Cold and steady. The kind that drowned without a ripple. The scars along his forearm heated until they throbbed. Each mark flared in warning, as if the air itself recognized its own kind.

He adjusted his coat and pulled his credentials from his pocket. A young officer, eyes hollow with exhaustion and too many night shifts, waved him through after a glance at the ID.

The alley was quiet now except for the crackle of radios and the low murmur of voices conferring over evidence bags.

Lena Kors sat slumped against the wall. Her throat had been cut clean through. The wound was precise and efficient. Blood had soaked the red bandana at her neck. Her dark curls were heavy with it, clinging to her pale skin.

An evidence bag lay beside her. Inside was a torn strip of dark fabric. The threads caught the light like tiny blue wires, shimmering faintly. Erik studied it, uncertain whether it was ordinary cloth or something woven with intent rather than thread alone. His jaw tightened.

The mark above her body glowed faintly under the floodlight, carved into the brick with deliberate precision. He had seen a similar symbol before. Several times now. Always the exact symmetry. Always drawn in blood. Always left like a signature demanding to be read. This one seemed slightly different, like something was missing, but it still carried energy it should not.

Erik pulled out his phone and took three photographs from different angles. He knew the photos would fail to show what mattered. The camera would not catch the shimmer or the way the lines appeared to breathe.

He crouched lower and let his senses open. The fire in his blood stirred, answering the energy still alive in the pattern. Not dragon work. The geometry was wrong. The curves were too deliberate, too human in their precision. But not entirely human either.

The old scars beneath his sleeve glowed softly, their heat rising with the pulse of the mark. They had always reacted to active magic, a relic from his first binding many years ago. Usually they ached like an old wound. Tonight they burned, as if answering a challenge.

He traced the air above the sigil without touching it. The residue pulsed against his palm like heat from a dying ember. Warm and insistent. Water-blessed. And beneath it all, something older that predated the Alliance's careful categories.

The killer was building toward something. Each death was a careful stroke in a larger design. He had seen too many rogue murders to mistake this for madness. Too clean. Too patient.

He stepped closer. The lines were steady. Confident. Carved without the tremor of hesitation. The edges held firm even where the brick was uneven. Whoever made this had control, the kind that came from practice or obsession. Yet the shape seemed to resist the air itself. The curves trembled faintly, as though the hand that drew them had fought against something unseen.

The scent of ash clashed with ozone. The heat beneath his skin climbed until his forearm felt ready to ignite. He clenched his fist until the sensation eased. He had trained too long to lose control here, to let fire answer without permission. He would need to come back later for a proper study. Too many eyes were on him now.

A voice broke through the murmur of the scene, sharp with authority. "Sir, you can't be here."

Erik turned. A detective stood near the tape, notepad in hand, his tie loose. Fatigue was etched into the corners of his eyes.

"Investigator Erik Varg," he said evenly. He reached into his coat and handed the man a plain white card.

Varg Investigations. Discreet Solutions.

"Detective Ben Hargrove," the man muttered. He flipped the card once before tucking it into his coat pocket. His gaze drifted to the body, then to the small evidence bag beside it. Without ceremony, he bent, picked it up, and slid it into his inner coat pocket with a practiced motion.

Erik's brow lifted slightly. No label. No note. No handoff to forensics.

"Who are you with?" Hargrove asked. His tone was flat. Almost bored.

"Private investigator," Erik said. He nodded toward the wall. "I work on pattern crimes. Families hire me when official cases go cold. Sometimes I consult with law enforcement when something connects to an active investigation."

The detective's mouth twisted in skepticism and exhaustion.

"Pattern crimes? What makes you think this connects to anything?"

"Third sigil like this in two months," Erik said. "Your captain called me in after the second one. Asked me to keep an eye out."

"Huh." Hargrove's pen tapped against his notepad. "We'll check the cameras, but it reads like a robbery gone bad to me."

His voice aimed for boredom, but his eyes kept drifting back to the sigil. Not in fear. Something closer to recognition. Like he had already filed it away and did not want to see it again.

Erik crouched beside the wall. The lines gleamed under his flashlight. Measured. Deliberate. Too precise for panic or improvisation. They pulsed faintly in time with his heart.

"This wasn't done in haste," he said quietly. "Whoever made this knew what they were doing. They wanted it to hold."

The detective's pen paused mid-note.

"You one of those pattern guys?"

Erik stood. His expression gave nothing.

"Close enough."

His eyes locked on the sigil. The glow in his scars pulsed in synchrony, in a way that made his chest tighten. The air around the wall trembled faintly. Hummed beneath the noise of radios. Vibrated with power that refused to settle. For a moment he thought he heard a whisper beneath the static. A slow breath. Patient. Waiting for an answer that had not yet been given.

26

Movement beyond the tape drew his attention like a magnet pulling at iron.

A woman stood there. Her blazer was stiff with blood. Her pendant glowed dimly against her chest. Her eyes were storm green, luminous in the flashing light. Rimmed in shadow. Wide with grief.

But it was not just grief in them. There was power. Old. Buried. Waking. It stirred behind her gaze like something ancient trying to rise. He had seen that look before, but only once. Mara.

He blinked, and for a heartbeat the resemblance hit like a blade. The same eyes, but not quite. Not just human. Not just memory. Her dragon had been quiet until now. Burning behind those storm-colored eyes. Faint but undeniable. And not just any dragon. Something older than training or lineage. Humming beneath her skin like pressure before a lightning strike.

She was active. And she did not know.

Recognition struck. His chest tightened. Heat rolled through him. His scars flared in response, their light answering something older that lived inside her presence. Something that called to the fire in his blood with undeniable certainty.

He did not understand it yet. Only that it was ancient and familiar. A connection that transcended logic or choice. He forced his breath steady. Suppressed the surge that threatened to break through. Logic faltered. Instinct whispered truths he was not ready to hear.

It struck deeper than thought. Older than breath. Not magic. Not prophecy. Just something older. Rarer. The kind of resonance that happened when dragon lines aligned too cleanly. Too fast.

He had never experienced it himself, but he had heard the stories. Bonds like this could build or destroy, depending on timing, strength, and control. Some described it like a magnet pulling under the skin. Others called it a storm looking for a mirror.

But nothing had prepared him for this.

As her eyes held his across the distance, a single thread of clarity cut through the noise.

She was Mara Grayson's sister.

And she was standing in the heart of a storm that had only begun.

CHAPTER 6

ALLIE

The alley buzzed with radios and boots on concrete. Red and blue light pulsed over wet brick. The air smelled of copper and ash.

Detective Hargrove stood near her, notepad open.

"Miss Grayson, I need you to walk me through what happened tonight."

Allie wrapped her arms around herself. Lena's blood had dried on her hands, dark and stiff.

"Lena called me at the office. Left a message saying she needed help. When I got to the bar, she seemed scared. Said she had something to tell me about my sister." Her voice cracked. "She wanted to close up first. I went to use the restroom. I heard her scream. I ran down the hallway and pushed through the back door. She was needing out right there in the alley."

Hargrove scribbled something.

"Did you see anyone?"

"A shadow. At the mouth of the alley. Tall. Wearing a coat. The light was behind him." Her hands trembled. "By the time I looked again, he was gone."

"And you called 911 immediately?"

"Yes. I tried to stop the bleeding, but there was so much." Her throat closed.

Hargrove's pen paused.

"I know this is hard, Miss Grayson. Just a few more questions."

Movement at the edge of her vision. Another man stood near the wall, studying the mark carved into the brick. He had not spoken since she arrived. Something about him made the air feel heavier.

"The mark on the wall," Hargrove said.

"Did you see it before or after you called for help?"

"Before. It was glowing." She knew how it sounded. "Like it was alive. And it looked exactly like the one I saw at my sister's accident three years ago."

Hargrove's expression went flat.

"Miss Grayson, you've been through a traumatic event. The mind can play tricks. Pattern recognition, visual distortion..."

"It wasn't a trick. I know what I saw."

"Blood spatter can create all kinds of shapes. Especially in low light."

"Detective."

The other man's voice cut through the noise. Quiet. Absolute.

Hargrove turned, irritation flickering across his face.

"Varg, I've got this."

The man stepped forward. His eyes found Allie's.

The pendant in her pocket flared hot. She gasped.

Across the alley, the man's jaw clenched. His hand flexed once.

The world narrowed. The noise faded. The lights blurred. Something hummed in the space between them.

Then a radio squawked.

Allie blinked. Her heart raced.

The man's expression stayed neutral, but tension coiled in his shoulders.

"Erik Varg," he said. His voice was steady. His eyes never left hers. "Private investigator. I've been looking into this pattern of crimes."

Pattern crimes. The words settled into her chest like a key finding a lock.

"You said it glowed," Erik said.

Allie nodded slowly.

"It pulsed. Like it had a heartbeat."

"Did it stop when you looked away?"

"Yes. How did you…"

"And Miss Kors gave you something before she died."

Not a question.

Allie's hand moved to her coat pocket. Lena's pendant lay warm and insistent.

"How do you know that?"

Erik's gaze dropped to her pocket. Something flickered in his eyes.

"Because this isn't the first time I've seen this."

Hargrove stepped between them.

"That's enough, Varg. You're here as a courtesy, not lead investigator." He turned to Allie.

"Miss Grayson, you've had a long night. We'll need a full statement tomorrow, but for now, go home. Get some rest. Someone from Victim Services will contact you."

Allie stared at him.

"That's it? You're letting me go?"

"Unless you're a suspect, yes. Right now, this looks like an interrupted robbery. Wrong place, wrong time. We'll pull camera footage, run forensics, and follow up in the morning."

"Robbery?" The word tasted wrong.

"She wasn't robbed. Her wallet was still in her apron. This was deliberate."

"The mark is blood spatter, Miss Grayson." Hargrove's voice had gone cold.

"I understand you're looking for answers, especially after what happened to your sister. But sometimes violence is just violence."

She turned away before she said something she would regret. As she moved toward the tape, Erik stepped into her path.

"Counsellor Grayson."

The way he said her name made her stop.

"You know who I am."

31

"I knew your sister. And I knew Lena. This was not random."

"Then tell the detective that."

"He would not listen." Something shifted in Erik's eyes. A warning.

"The sigil on that wall is the fourth I've seen in the last few years. Each one marks a murder. Each victim had ties to old bloodlines. Your sister. Lena. Others."

Old bloodlines. The phrase sent ice down her spine.

"What does that mean?"

"It means someone's hunting." He glanced at Hargrove, then back to her.

"And whoever killed Lena knows you were here. They saw you."

The shadow in the alley. The way it had watched her.

"Why are you telling me this?"

"Because you're in danger. And because the detective is wrong. This won't stop with Lena."

Before she could respond, Hargrove called out.

"Varg, I need you over here."

Erik held her gaze for one more moment. Then he stepped back into the shadows.

Allie stood alone beneath the yellow tape. Her hands shook. Lena's pendant pulsed warm in her pocket.

She turned and walked away from the alley, from the flashing lights, from the mark on the wall that Hargrove refused to see.

Erik's words followed her into the dark.

This won't stop with Lena.

And deep down, she knew he was right.

CHAPTER 7

ERIK

The alley narrowed as the uniforms began to clear out. Sirens faded into the distance. The sound of boots gave way to the softer rustle of plastic bags, the clipped zip of evidence kits being sealed. The scent of blood lingered in the air, metallic and stubborn.

Erik remained where he was, just beyond the edge of the yellow tape. He watched Allie disappear into the traffic beyond. Her blazer was stiff with blood, dark along the sleeves and across her shoulders. Her steps faltered once, but she kept her head high. Her jaw was set. She refused to break until she was out. He recognized that kind of strength. Not pride. Survival. The same armor he had worn for years. When she vanished around the corner, he let out a slow breath. The glow from the sigil had faded completely, but its residue still curled beneath his skin. Old magic lingered in the bones of the alley.

He crouched again near the wall and ignored the glance from a rookie officer gathering evidence markers. The mark carved into the brick remained sharp and precise. Each line was deliberate. Not a madman's scribble. Whoever had made it understood what they were doing. They understood the geometry and the cost. That unsettled him more than the death it accompanied.

He reached out and let his fingers hover just above the surface. The air shimmered faintly. His scars warmed beneath his sleeve. The sigil had been alive earlier, and it had tasted something it liked.

He rose as Detective Hargrove approached from the other end of the alley. The detective's coat was dusted with grime. His jaw was set in tired frustration.

"You finished here?" Hargrove asked. "The DA's team will process the rest in the morning."

Erik gave a quiet nod. "You won't get much from forensics."

"Excuse me?"

"By sunrise the pattern will be gone. It always is."

The detective squinted at him. Suspicion crept into his expression. "You sound very sure."

"I've seen this before."

"Where?"

Erik looked at him without blinking. "You wouldn't believe me."

Hargrove exhaled, low and frustrated. He walked off, muttering into his radio about consultants who thought they knew everything.

Erik turned back to the wall. The alley had quieted, though a few bystanders lingered beyond the barrier. They smoked or watched with pale curiosity. A cyclist coasted by without stopping, earbuds in, oblivious. City life reasserted itself slowly.

He could still hear the edge in Allie's voice, the way she described the sigil's glow. Pulsing. Alive. Exactly as it had been. Most witnesses forgot what they saw within hours. But not her. Her memory had held. Her pendant had answered. That made her rare. Possibly dangerous. Possibly vital. Definitely vulnerable.

Erik walked back to his truck.

He sat in the driver's seat with the door open, one foot still on the pavement. The dashboard clock showed 1:23 a.m. Friday morning, technically. He stayed there for a long moment. The pendant. The woman's eyes. The way the sigil had pulsed in recognition.

He had seen bonds form before. He knew the signs. The heat. The pull. The sense that something had clicked into place that could not be

34

undone. But never this fast. Never this strong. And never with someone who had no idea what she was.

The danger was not the bond itself, but her ignorance of it. She would not know to shield. She would not know to hide. The moment her power truly woke, every dragon in the city would feel it. And the Watchers would come.

He pulled out his phone and scrolled to Torvald's number. He hesitated, then pressed call. The line picked up on the second ring.

"Tell me you're not still in Deep Ellum," Torvald said. His voice was rough. "The locals don't take kindly to poachers."

"I'm off the clock," Erik said. "Just getting a read on the scene. It was too messy with Dallas PD hovering."

"That mess being a murder scene?"

Erik leaned back against the headrest. "Lena Kors. Multiple stab wounds. Mark on the wall that looked like a sigil, but the strokes were wrong."

"Wrong how?"

"Too clean," Erik said. "Not the usual rogue work. There is intent here, but not one of ours. Could be mimicry, or something older." He rubbed at the scar beneath his sleeve. "It looked incomplete. Under-powered, maybe, but still active. The witness might've interrupted him. It hummed though. Like the others."

Torvald grunted. "Then it is connected."

"Maybe. Or maybe someone wants it to look that way."

"Witness?"

"Allie Grayson," Erik said quietly.

The line went still. "Grayson," Torvald repeated. "Does that name ring any bells for you?"

"Yes," Erik said softly. "Mara's younger sister."

Torvald exhaled. "Did she see the murder?"

"No. She saw him from a distance as he was leaving, but no clear view."

"You did not tell her anything?"

"Of course not."

"Did she see anything unusual?"

Erik hesitated. "No, she was just shaken. Mara died three years ago tomorrow."

The lie came easier than he expected. He was not sure why he said it, only that some part of him did not want Torvald to know about her dragon yet. If a bond was involved, it was his problem, not the Alliance's.

Torvald went quiet. "So what is your read on the killer? Rogue?"

Erik's eyes drifted toward the alley. "If it was a rogue, they've learned to write with purpose. The sigil had weight. Ritual symmetry. But the lines, one curved where it should've split. Water, not fire. Different from the others."

"That is still a connection."

"Or evolution," Erik said. "Either way, I'm not calling it yet. I want to check the other sites tomorrow and see if the pattern holds."

Torvald sighed. "Send me the data and go home. If it's not a rogue, it's not your case."

Erik smirked faintly, though there was no humor in it. "And miss all the fun?"

"This is not fun," Torvald muttered. "This is how hunters burn out. You remember Thompson?"

The name hung between them. Erik remembered. Thompson had chased a pattern for six months straight. No sleep. No backup. He had been convinced he was close. They found what was left of him in a warehouse off Highway 80. His body had been burned so hot that the concrete beneath him had cracked.

"Yes," Erik said finally. "I remember."

He hung up before Torvald could respond.

The silence that followed felt heavier than the call itself. He rubbed his temples. The ghost of a headache formed behind his eyes.

He slid the phone onto the dash and shut the door. Inside, the air felt cooler, scrubbed clean by the AC. After the alley's stink, it hit sharp and dry.

Lena was gone. Another dragon carved out of the city. He had known her, not well, but enough that it should not feel this routine. A streetcar rumbled in the distance. A bell chimed once. The world moved on, as it always did.

Erik stared across the rooftops. Somewhere out there, the killer had already moved on. Washing blood from gloved hands. Choosing the next name. The shape of the sigil remained in his memory. Wrong. Deliberate. Evolving. This was not simple ritual. Someone was building something, and each death was another brick in a structure he could not yet see. She might be marked whether she knew it or not. And Allie Grayson was standing at its center.

His scars flared again. Heat crawled up his arm. He had trained himself to ignore pain, to burn without flinching, to let fire move through him without losing control. A bent saxophone note drifted from a nearby bar.

He started the engine and pulled away from Deep Ellum. The city lights blurred past. Neon reflected in puddles. His phone buzzed twice with Alliance updates he did not read.

Erik did not look back.

CHAPTER 8

ALLIE

The alley felt colder now that the questions had stopped. The radios had gone quiet, the sharp rhythm of boots fading into the street beyond. Silence settled over her.

Allie stood alone beneath the flickering security light. Her breath rose in small clouds. The scent of blood clung to her hands. When she turned to look back, the wall where the sigil had burned held only a dull smear of red. Just blood. Just brick.

Lena's face flashed behind her eyes. Pale. Still. Blood spreading dark beneath her. Her breath caught.

She raised her hand for a cab near the corner. The driver unlocked the door. She slid into the back seat. Gave her address. Turned toward the window. Streetlights passed.

The cab stopped outside her apartment. Her fingers fumbled with the bills. Dropped one. Picked it up. Pressed cash into the driver's hand. The driver said something. She did not hear it.

Inside, the stairwell was silent. She leaned against her apartment door until the hallway steadied. Then she let herself in. Coffee grounds and worn books. Too quiet. Too empty.

One lamp lit the kitchen. Long shadows across the table where her briefcase should have been. The space beside the chair was empty. Her heart sank. The hearing was scheduled for the morning. Her notes, the file, all of it left behind at the bar.

She pressed her fingers to her brow. Hargrove's voice in her head, dismissive and tired. She closed her eyes. Not tonight.

The blood on her hands. Crusted in her cuticles. Smudged across her wrists. Dark beneath her fingernails. She gripped the sink. Turned on the tap. Scrubbed until her skin burned red. Pink water spiraled down the drain.

She wandered back to the kitchen. Stood where her briefcase should have been. A spare key. Did she still have one? She opened the drawer. Tugged roughly. Retrieved the ring. Keys jingled. One caught the light. Brass. Tag worn thin. She tilted it under the bulb. BCL. Black Cat Lounge.

She dropped into the nearest chair and pulled the pendant from her coat pocket. A faint blue shimmer passed through it. The pulse slowed. Faded. Her thumb traced the broken chain, blackened near the clasp. Heat spread in her palm, radiating to her fingers. She closed her hand around it. Closed her eyes.

"Lena," she whispered. "What'd you know?"

No answer. Only the refrigerator's hum. Outside, another siren wailed into the distance.

The mark on the wall. Pulsing. Moving. Like something alive.

Her limbs felt heavy. She crossed to the table and set Lena's pendant down beside the small photo of Mara. The two of them on a pier, wind in their hair. Then, almost without thinking, she unclasped her own chain. The one Eleanor had pressed into her hand at the funeral three years earlier. Whispered that Mara would have wanted her to have it. She laid it beside the other.

The pendants were nearly identical. Lena's was brighter, slightly larger. The etchings sharp, untouched by time. Mara's pendant showed its age. Initials still visible, MG carved neatly into the back. Links darkened, bent where time had twisted them. Etchings softened, worn down.

She blinked hard. Fought the tears. The questions could wait.

Tomorrow she would pull the files. Call the bar. Make sense of it. Tonight, she would breathe.

The two pendants lay side by side. Silver edges caught the low light. Then, with no wind or movement, Lena's pendant shimmered once more. The light from its core pulsed slowly. Faded.

She turned off the lamp and walked toward the bedroom.

Behind her in the shadowed quiet, the broken chain stirred. A single link shifted with a faint metallic click. It sealed itself closed.

The room fell silent again, but something unseen had changed.

CHAPTER 9

ERIK

*A*cross the street, Erik stood beneath a flickering streetlight. Mist clung to his coat. His hands stayed buried in his pockets. It was nearly two in the morning. The city had quieted to a low hum.

Before ending his day, he had to check on Allie. He called the Trial Bureau answering service. They picked up after two rings. He gave the badge number tied to his current cover and explained that he needed Counselor Grayson's home address for a follow-up. The woman barely hesitated, read it off to him. He thanked her and hung up.

Now he stood outside the apartment building, watching the faint glow behind the third-floor window. The light was still on. That meant she had not yet slept. Neither had he.

He should have walked away. The case did not belong to him. The Alliance had clear rules about witness contact, and he had already broken two tonight. The forged credentials were only the beginning. Withholding information from Torvald was another violation entirely. But his connection to the victims, and now to Allie, and that sigil on the wall had changed everything.

Its shape haunted him. Even now, he could feel its pattern like heat pressed into his spine. Not just old. Forbidden. That symbol belonged to the blood rites buried after the elemental wars, rites outlawed when storm and fire nearly leveled three cities and drowned a fourth. Those glyphs had been sealed for a reason, their knowledge scattered and destroyed. No one alive should be able to draw them. No one should remember how.

His jaw locked tight. He closed his eyes and focused on the flicker behind his ribs. The fire in his veins stirred, slow, watchful. Fire meets storm. He had never felt the bond before, but some things needed only a heartbeat to be known. The old words burned in his memory. Every Alliance hunter learned the Prophecy of the Six in training. Most dismissed it as folklore. Erik had stopped dismissing anything three years ago. Now fire watches. That was what disturbed him most.

He looked again at the apartment window three stories up. A soft light still glowed behind the curtain. The pull inside him deepened, not attraction but something older. It vibrated behind his scars, a rhythm he could not name. He felt like a stalker, standing in the dark and watching her window. He hated the bond for making him feel that way. The killer had seen her. Not clearly, maybe, but enough to know she was there. Enough for her presence to fracture the sigil. That alone made her a variable the killer would not ignore.

The light in her window flickered once, and his mind drifted backward.

Lena's face rose again in his memory. Not pale and still in that alley, but alive, angry, pleading. They had met once, almost a decade ago. Erik had been sent to pull William Kors out of Dragon's Breath, a mixed Watcher and Dragon band that toured on the eastern edge of Denton County.

William had gone too long without using his water power. The magic had built up past safe levels, pressurized inside him like steam behind glass. He had begun to unravel. Flashes of sudden floods, emotional volatility, tremors in his aura. Another week, maybe two, and he would have gone full rogue. The water storms alone would have made national news.

Lena had been there. She had shown up after the Alliance flagged the containment order. She had not come with a weapon. She had come as a daughter. Erik remembered the way she had cornered him outside the extraction site, jaw set, ready to fight if he gave the wrong answer.

"Are you going to kill him?" she had asked.

"No," he had answered. "Not if I can help it."

She had studied him for a long moment before nodding. "Do better than talk. Help him drain it off."

Erik had convinced the Alliance to place William in protected isolation, not termination. With time, careful channeling, and supervised release work, the man had stabilized. The last Erik heard, William had taken up gardening. But Lena had remained cautious. Like most dragons, she had seen too many decisions made in the name of control. She knew the Alliance would choose containment over compassion if it came to that. She did not distrust Erik, but she distrusted what he worked for.

And now she was gone. Another name carved out of the city.

A shadow passed behind the curtain above him, pausing near what might have been a table. When it vanished deeper into the apartment, he exhaled and stepped back from the curb.

He checked the block again, scanning doorways and parked cars. No watchers, no engines idling, no shimmer of spellcraft beneath the streetlamps. The shadows lay flat and ordinary. Only then did his shoulders ease.

He turned down the sidewalk. His boots tapped against damp concrete, each step muffled by the mist that had settled low over the street.

By morning, he would file a clean report. No mention of sigil resonance. No record of her pendant answering his scars. No notes about the sudden tether between them that hummed like a live wire. That part would stay buried.

Because this story had not started tonight. This was the middle of something that began years ago, perhaps centuries, if the sigil was what he feared it was. And whatever curse had surfaced again, it had chosen its players carefully.

Behind him the street swallowed his steps.

By the time he parked outside his apartment building, the dashboard clock showed 2:14 a.m. He climbed the stairs slowly, made coffee he would not drink, and opened his notebook to begin mapping what he knew.

The symbols stared back at him from the page, refusing to make sense.

Sleep could wait. The pattern could not.

CHAPTER 10

ALLIE

*A*t 2:37 a.m., Allie gave up on sleep.

Sheets twisted around her legs, knotted from hours of turning. Time had stopped making sense the moment the blade struck. Her body was bone-tired, thoughts circling the same loop. The alley. The blood. The way Lena's hand had gone slack in hers. Every muscle ached. Her eyes burned. Sleep refused to come.

She walked into the kitchen. Bare feet cold against tile. A car passed outside. The refrigerator hummed. On the table, the two pendants caught the glow of a distant streetlight. She had avoided touching Lena's since leaving the bar. The flare of light. The heat. The way it had locked her hand in place. Yet now, drawn by something she could not name, her hand reached for it.

The chain slipped between her fingers. Cool. Smooth. The pendant pressed against her skin. It pulsed once, a soft throb like a heartbeat answering her own. She jerked back. It had pulsed. Not her imagination. Real. And the broken chain was whole.

She stared at the window's black reflection. For a moment, she saw Mara instead. That crooked grin. The last time they had spoken was at the lake. Mara had worn that same pendant then, the metal catching sunlight.

"This is not real," she whispered. "Shock. Trauma. Grief playing tricks."

Her eyes landed on the keyring beside her wallet. The small brass key still had a tag etched with BCL. Black Cat Lounge. The hearing was scheduled for eight o'clock. The briefcase with all her prep work still sat in Lena's office, forgotten the moment Lena had fallen. Morrison would crucify her if she showed up empty-handed. Three weeks of preparation tucked into navy leather. She had a reason to go back. A rational, defensible reason.

She grabbed her shoes, tugged on her jacket, and called for a cab. While she waited, she washed her face in the bathroom sink. Cold water shocked her skin awake. Her reflection looked haunted. Dark circles beneath red-rimmed eyes. Hair tangled. She tied it back and did not look again.

The cab pulled up. She stepped into the mist and hurried to it. Her heart thudded against her ribs. Water dotted the sidewalk, cold and sharp.

The city passed in fragments as the cab wound through empty streets. Neon reflected in puddles. Windows glowed briefly before vanishing. She kept her hands folded tight in her lap. Nails dug crescents into her palms.

"You sure about this address, Miss?" the driver asked. He slowed at a familiar corner. His eyes found hers in the rearview mirror.

They had reached Deep Ellum. Bars had gone dark hours ago. Only closed storefronts and graffiti remained.

"I'm sure," she said, though her voice sounded thin.

The cab rolled toward Elm Street. Police tape sagged at the alley's mouth. Wind tugged it softly. A police cruiser pulled away as she stepped out. Taillights disappeared. She was alone with the silence.

She paid the driver and approached the side entrance slowly. Her hand shook as she slipped the key into the lock. It turned with a soft click.

Inside, the silence hit hard. No music. No laughter. Just the low hum of the soda machine. The air held faint traces of cleaner and citrus. Something scrubbed away.

She made her way to Lena's office. Each step careful. Her heart drummed louder than her shoes on the hardwood. Shadows pooled in corners. The emergency exit sign cast everything in red.

The door stood open. The overhead light snapped on with a buzz that made her flinch.

There it was. Her briefcase. Navy leather damp with cold air. She grabbed it. Relief flooded through her.

Her hands steadier now. Lawyer instincts took over. Evidence. Questions. Patterns. She scanned the office, looking for whatever Lena had wanted her to see.

A sound behind her. Soft. A hinge settled. A frame shifted. She stilled. Every nerve went alert.

She opened the office door and stepped into the bar's main room. The space looked undisturbed. Tables sat empty. Glasses gleamed on shelves. One stool near the end rocked faintly.

"Hello?" Her voice felt small.

No answer. Only the hum of the cooler and the distant drip of a faucet.

From somewhere outside, a saxophone moaned. One long note. Not recorded. Live. Someone was playing in the street at four in the morning.

She moved through the dark, one hand brushing the edges of tables. Her briefcase hung heavy at her side. At the exit, she paused. The saxophone had stopped.

The alley was empty when she looked. Neon flickered on the walls. The air smelled of wet brick. Police tape fluttered where it had torn loose. She stepped out and locked the door. Her hands fumbled with the key.

Then she saw it. Caught against the doorframe, wedged where the tape had pulled free. A matchbook. Black paper. Silver lettering gleamed in the neon. *Dragon's Breath.*

She picked it up carefully. The paper was dry. A chill chased up her arms.

The logo was unfamiliar, but something about it twisted in her gut. No address printed inside. No phone number. Just a spiral, drawn by hand in silver ink. Delicate. Precise.

Beneath it was a string of numbers, handwritten. It looked like Lena's handwriting.

32.7401. -96.8282.

Coordinates. Or a code.

She turned it over. The back was blank, except for one word, so faint she almost missed it: *Midnight.*

Making no sense of it, she slid the matchbook into her briefcase and walked quickly to her car, half a block away in shadow.

The keys trembled in her hand as she unlocked the door and slid inside. She locked it immediately.

Her chest heaved.

The drive home blurred together. Water traced lines across the windshield. She drove on autopilot, muscle memory guiding her through turns she barely registered.

She parked in front of her building and sat. Engine running. Breath fogging the glass. The steering wheel still warm beneath her palms. Outside, the street was empty.

Inside, the apartment was still too quiet. The clock read 3:41 a.m. She hung her coat on the hook and dropped the briefcase on the table beside the pendants. She stared at her hands under the kitchen light. The soap had not removed all the blood. Dark crescents remained beneath her nails.

She undressed slowly in the bathroom. Each button a burden. Her clothes smelled like the bar. Smoke and lemon and something metallic. She dropped them in the hamper and turned the shower on full. Waited for steam to fill the space.

When the water hit her, she broke. The sobs came. Not only Lena. Mara. The guardrail. The pendant. The sigil. All of it. She slid down the tile wall until the water ran cold.

Later, wrapped in a towel with her hair dripping, she stood before the fogged mirror. Her hand wiped a circle clear. Her face looked hollow. Eyes red and swollen. Skin pale. Hair damp and wild.

She dropped onto the bed without changing. Without drying off. The sheets were cold against her skin. The clock read 4:12 a.m. Her body ached in ways sleep would not fix. Her mind was finally, mercifully quiet.

Sleep took her before she could resist.

In her dreams, she heard the saxophone again. And beneath it, a voice calling her name.

CHAPTER 11

KILLER

a basement. Concrete walls. A single bare bulb.

Four sigils lined the eastern wall. Three were complete, painted in shades of blood that had dried to black. The fourth remained fractured, its edges broken where the storm-touched had interrupted the work.

They pressed a palm to the newest mark. No heat radiated back.

The pattern had shattered when she appeared in the alley. The sigil refused to hold.

Blood had dried past the wrist.

The serpent-hilted knife rested on the floor beside them.

They stared at the broken lines.

Repair would require more than blood. More than will. Another offering. Another death.

* * *

ACROSS THE CITY, another room.

Third floor. Street noise filtered through thin walls.

Four identical sigils covered the northern wall, painted on wood paneling. Three complete. One fractured.

53

A hand reached out, pressing against the broken pattern.

Nothing. No pulse. No response.

They withdrew. The fourth would have to wait. Five and six first. Then return to repair the damage.

* * *

IN THE BASEMENT, a finger traced the fractured edges.

The geometry was sound. The blood was real.

But the power had drained the moment she touched her pendant.

Storm calling to storm, breaking what should have been sealed.

* * *

ON THE THIRD FLOOR, they stepped back from the wall.

The plan had not changed. Only the order.

Five would come next. Then six.

Then the fourth could be completed properly, with the power of all six feeding into the circle.

But something else pulled at them.

The scene had been rushed.

The storm-touched had interrupted before the work was done.

In the chaos, something had been left behind. Small, but enough.

They had recovered it before anyone else noticed, but still, a thread that could unravel if pulled.

They forced the thought away.

The ache in their chest remained.

Sleep came rarely now.

And when it did, they dreamed of scales splitting skin.

They dreamed of cities on fire.

* * *

IN THE BASEMENT, they wiped the blade clean.

The rag was stiff with old blood.

The body did not matter. Only the mark.

Only the pattern carved into stone and brick, feeding the chain that had been broken three centuries ago.

* * *

ON THE THIRD FLOOR, the window creaked open.

Cold air rushed in.

Below, the city pulsed with light and noise, unaware of what moved beneath its streets.

Unaware of what had begun to wake.

The storm-touched in the alley had worn a pendant.

They had seen it glow when she knelt beside the body.

Seen the way it flared in recognition.

She was marked.

Whether she knew it or not.

* * *

IN THE BASEMENT, the candle on the workbench flickered once and fell still.

On the third floor, the streetlight outside the window buzzed, then dimmed.

* * *

TWO ROOMS. Two hands.

One pattern rising in the dark.

The fourth could be repaired.

The fifth mark would come soon.

And the sixth would follow.

Then, with the full circle complete, the binding would break.

Six marks to wake the chain.

Six deaths to shatter what had held for three hundred years.

And when the storm-touched finally understood what she carried, it would already be too late.

CHAPTER 12

ERIK

*E*rik sat in his truck outside a diner on Commerce Street. A black notebook lay open on the dash. His coffee had gone cold beside it. Five hours had passed since the Black Cat Lounge. He was running on caffeine and momentum.

The notebook was filled with sketches. Glyphs. Partial translations. Names in three ancient tongues. He had drawn the mark from the alley four times and still could not capture it correctly.

It was not identical to the others. The previous two had formed perfect symmetry, circles sealed and complete. This one fractured at the base, leaving a gap. Deliberate. Not error, but intent. He could not yet tell which.

Erik studied the map on his phone. Four murder sites were marked with red pins. They traced a pattern. With the fourth sigil, the lines had begun to curve. The killer was not just carving marks. They were forging a circuit.

His phone buzzed. Torvald.

Erik answered. "Morning."

Torvald's voice rasped. "Morning my ass. Have you looked at the report yet?"

"Which one?"

"Hargrove's statement came in an hour ago. They're calling it a robbery gone wrong."

Erik smiled without warmth. "Of course they are."

Silence followed. Then, "The survivor. The Grayson woman. She's clean?"

"She's a lawyer. Corporate cases. Fresh out of school."

"Lawyer," Torvald echoed flatly.

"She doesn't understand what she saw. Her mind's trying to rationalize it."

"Then let it. You know the rules. No witness contact unless sanctioned by Command."

"That rule exists for people who panic. She's not panicking. She's thinking."

"That's worse."

Outside, a city bus rumbled past.

Torvald's tone eased. "Look, I know what you think this is. But these glyphs deviate from the old records."

"I noticed." Erik studied the fractured rune.

"So drop it. If it's a rogue cultist, cleanup will handle them. If it's deeper, Command handles it."

Erik traced the jagged line splitting the glyph. Command had decided ten years ago that the curse had faded, the threat buried. The Council of Five had voted. The old wars were over, they said. Move on. Erik had never believed it.

"One more thing," Torvald said. "Command flagged it yesterday. Three Watcher sightings in Dallas over six months."

Erik's grip tightened. "They're usually ghosts."

"That's the worry. Sloppy, or scheming?"

"You link them to the kills?"

"Sigils flaring in sequence? That's Watcher bait. They guard the curse. If someone's prying it apart, they'd crush it. Bodies be damned."

"Even hers."

"Exactly. Watch your back. And keep that civilian out. If Watchers mark her as anything..." Torvald did not finish. The line died.

Erik stared at the phone, then flipped the notebook open. He traced the broken circle again. Not identical. Not random.

Dragon deaths made noise. They were rare. Dragons were careful. Most could vanish or shield before trouble found them. But when a dragon died unusually, it sent a pulse through their community. When it was murder, when it bore a sigil, it rang out.

Erik flipped to the beginning of his notebook. The timeline stared back.

July 2018, Milo Garran, earth element, perfect symmetry, ruled work accident.

October 2022, Mara Grayson, air element, perfect symmetry, vehicular accident.

Three months ago, Carlos Mendez, fire element, disappeared, no sigil confirmed.

Last night, Lena Kors, water element, third confirmed sigil, but fractured.

The pattern broke when Allie Grayson interfered.

Two complete. One broken. One unconfirmed. Two remaining.

He turned to a blank page and wrote in block letters: Earth. Air. Water. Fire? Storm? Spirit?

Six marks to wake the chain.

Too precise for chance. Someone was invoking the ancient balance, or trying to break it.

He circled each in red, lines connecting them. In the margin he wrote: Two left?

His gaze lifted to the windshield. Morning fog blurred the skyline.

He snapped the notebook shut and tucked it into his coat. Time to see what Allie Grayson meant in this storm.

He started the engine and merged into traffic, heading east toward the courthouse. Counselor Grayson would be in session soon.

Behind him, the morning light stretched across the glass towers.

CHAPTER 13

ALLIE

The alarm had been screaming for three minutes before Allie finally silenced it. Her body felt heavy. Unwilling to move.

She showered on autopilot. Hair still damp when she emerged. The night had emptied her out. Getting up was harder today, but necessary.

She returned to find the pendants still on the table where she had left them.

She reached for her pendant, Mara's, the tarnished one she had worn every day for three years. Her hand hesitated. A strange reluctance. She blinked it away, blamed exhaustion, and reached again.

Her fingers found chain and metal. She did not look down as she fastened it. The clasp closed with a soft click.

It was not until she glanced in the mirror that something felt off. The pendant looked brighter than she remembered. But that was only the morning light.

She turned away before the thought could settle.

On the table behind her, the tarnished pendant with faint initials lay beside Mara's photograph, exactly where she had left it.

She dressed quickly. Otherwise she would be late for court.

Coffee steadied her hands but not her thoughts. The taste was

61

bitter and metallic. By the time she locked the door and stepped outside, the city had begun to stir. Routine, she told herself, was survival.

The morning light glimmered too brightly against the mist-soaked pavement. Every sound carried farther than it should have. The hum of a car engine thrummed through her bones. When a crow burst from a power line, the flutter of its wings rippled in her chest.

She blinked, startled. The world steadied, but only just. Her heart-beat matched the rhythm of her pendant, each pulse warm enough to feel.

She climbed into her car and started the engine. The headlights caught the mist still clinging to the street. For a moment, the droplets shimmered pale blue. She rubbed her eyes and told herself it was fatigue.

The drive to the courthouse felt longer than usual. The city's noises layered together in strange harmony. Beneath it all was something she could not name, a vibration, subtle but constant.

By the time she pulled into the courthouse garage, the world looked normal again. Normal enough to pretend. But as she reached for her briefcase, the pendant under her blouse pulsed once, a single throb of warmth against her heart.

She exhaled slowly, locked the car, and headed toward the court-house steps.

The courthouse felt colder than usual. The marble steps gleamed with leftover mist, and the air inside carried a ghost of coffee, toner, and something sharper. Her heels echoed across the polished floor, each click reverberating longer than it should have.

When she pushed through the double doors of the courtroom, her nerves settled into the familiar choreography of duty. She had done this hundreds of times. Today, it all felt slightly out of sync.

Allie found her seat near the front, setting her briefcase at her feet. Her hands still trembled slightly. Routine was control.

The judge entered. Allie stood automatically, but her eyes caught something impossible. Behind him, for a moment, a thread of shimmer traced the air, a glint of blue light. She blinked and it vanished.

She sat again, forcing her focus to the case. Ordinary things. Familiar rhythms. Yet nothing felt familiar.

The fluorescent lights hummed. Suddenly she could hear each individual filament vibrating. Not just hear, but feel them, tiny threads brushing against her skin. Her breath shortened.

She gripped the table's edge. The judge's voice reached her strangely. Outside, water began to fall, and each drop that struck the window sent a pulse through her bones.

She tried to breathe slowly. Her pen. She forced herself to reach for it, gripping it tightly. Her other hand went to her throat, pressing the pendant through her blouse.

It was warmer than usual. Heavier. Had it always been this heavy?

She pushed the thought away. Grief made everything feel strange.

But the pendant pulsed against her palm, insistent, and for a moment she could have sworn she heard a voice whisper, *Be still.*

Her fingers loosened without her permission. Her hand was cold. So cold it hurt.

She dropped the pen. It clattered across the notepad, leaving a trail of frost that melted almost immediately. No one else reacted. No one saw.

The pendant under her blouse throbbed steadily now, constant, like a second heartbeat. It was warm while her hands were freezing.

Mara, what is happening to me?

Her pen hovered above the notepad. She pressed it to the paper, desperate to ground herself. But the lines curved, bending into arcs that resembled the sigil from the alley. The sight froze her hand.

Then she noticed it. A drop of water rested on the page, perfectly round. It did not move. It did not soak into the paper. And then it vanished. No trace.

Her pulse jumped.

A sharp sound cut through the air. For a moment she thought she heard the saxophone again, that same melody, threading beneath the judge's voice.

She closed her eyes and forced a steady breath. The sound faded.

Her gaze drifted to the back row and stopped. Erik Varg.

He sat half in shadow, coat collar turned up, expression unreadable. The overhead lights flickered once.

Their eyes met. The world snapped into focus.

Her hand flew to the pendant pressing against her chest. It was burning, not with heat but with cold that felt like fire. The metal seared against her skin, but when she tried to pull it away, it would not budge.

She looked down. The pendant blazed with pale blue light beneath her blouse. But no one turned. No one stared. The light was only for her.

She pressed her palm over it. The moment her skin touched the metal, a jolt shot through her, not pain exactly but recognition.

The pendant pulsed in rhythm with her heartbeat. Only it was not quite her rhythm. It stumbled once, caught a beat that was not hers, then steadied again.

"Counselor Grayson," the judge said.

Her head jerked up. "Yes, Your Honor."

The light returned to normal. She realized she was gripping her pen so tightly her knuckles had gone white.

"You are quiet today."

Her throat was dry. "Late night."

He nodded and continued. She forced her mind back to the table. Routine was survival.

When the recess was called, she gathered her papers too quickly. One file slipped and hit the floor, pages scattering.

She bent to retrieve them, and her fingers brushed something warm. A business card, plain white stock.

Erik Varg. A phone number. Nothing else.

She looked up, scanning the courtroom. He was gone. The back row where he had been sitting was empty.

She turned the card over. Blank.

Her fingers closed around it, and she slipped it into her coat pocket.

She straightened and made her way into the hall.

The corridor smelled of lemon polish and ozone. She leaned against the wall, her pulse thundering. The pendant under her blouse was warm again.

Her phone buzzed. A news alert.

WFAA Local: Police Investigation into Deep Ellum Homicide – A Robbery.

The thumbnail showed the Black Cat sign, the alley sealed with tape. She clicked it. For an instant she thought she saw something etched into the wall above the crime scene, something glowing where blood had been scrubbed away. The same curling lines.

She locked her phone and pressed it to her chest. She needed air.

The corridor echoed with footsteps and quiet conversation. She walked fast, papers hugged tight to her chest.

"Counselor Grayson."

She startled.

Detective Hargrove stood near the elevator bank, dressed in a dark suit, no badge in sight. A file was tucked under one arm.

"Detective." She stopped. Her voice came out thinner than intended.

He nodded. "Tough morning?"

"I'm fine," she said quickly. Too quickly.

"Why are you here?"

"Testimony on a case. Just passing through." He paused. "You look pale. You sure you're well?"

She shifted her weight, suddenly aware of the pendant's warmth. "Yes. Thank you."

He stepped aside to let her pass, but his eyes followed her. "Take care, Miss Grayson."

The courthouse doors swung shut behind her. Outside, the city blazed under a washed sky, light scattering off every wet surface.

She crossed the plaza steps slowly. The city's rhythm had changed. Even the wind seemed to carry whispers.

For a moment music rose. A saxophone. Low, mournful, alive.

The melody was familiar, the same restless rise and fall she had heard before. She turned toward the sound.

Across the plaza, under the striped awning of a coffee cart, the saxophonist played with her eyes closed. Morning light glinted off the brass, and for an instant Allie thought she saw a flicker of gold in the woman's gaze as she opened them.

The tune shifted, sliding from melancholy to something more deliberate. A warning disguised as music.

Allie froze. The pendant under her collarbone warmed, its pulse keeping time with the rhythm.

Then the music softened, dissolving into an ordinary street melody. The moment passed.

She blinked. The saxophone's tone had changed, back to a street song.

Someone brushed past her shoulder. She exhaled.

"Get a grip," she whispered. "You're imagining it."

The sound followed her as she crossed the street to the parking garage. By the time she reached her car, her pulse had found its own rhythm to match it.

She slid behind the wheel and shut the door. Silence rushed in, too sudden.

The pendant resting near her heart was warm again, steady. She glanced toward the plaza through the windshield. The woman was gone.

A horn blared behind her. She jumped. The car in her rearview mirror flashed its lights impatiently.

She swallowed hard. She was done pretending. She needed answers. Today.

She started the engine and pulled out into traffic, eyes fixed on the road, refusing to look back.

CHAPTER 14

KILLER

The courtyard was busy. Color. Sound. Sunlight glinting off wet stone. Pigeons circled above.

They stood in the shadow beneath the arcade, motionless, the hood of their coat drawn low. The crowd moved around them, unseeing.

She was there. The lawyer. The storm-eyed woman.

Light clung to her skin, a shimmer only they could see. It stirred the voice inside.

The tether breathes. Take her. Now.

They stepped forward. Measured the distance. Twenty steps. But the music reached them first.

A saxophone drifted from the far side of the plaza, low and restless. Each note sharp. The sound brushed their skin and burned.

The voice recoiled. Hissed.

Not her. The serpent guards her.

Pain lanced behind their eyes. The melody pressed deeper, scattering pigeons into the sky. Old magic woven into sound. Dragon song meant to ward, to banish.

The crowd heard only jazz. They heard a binding older than the curse itself.

They turned away, breath shallow, vision bright with pain. The sigils hidden beneath their clothes stirred, itching toward heat.

Once hidden, they pressed both hands to their face. Beneath the skin, bones shifted.

The curse had chosen them for the raw magic in their blood. Not dragon. Not Watcher. Morna-born. A conduit. But vessels crack under pressure.

We are running out of time. Finish the circle. Then we're free.

"Then we're free," the killer said. But whose voice was it now?

When the music finally stopped, they pressed a bloodied hand to the nearest window. The reflection shimmered, and for an instant the glass showed not just their own face but another overlaid atop it. Their partner. Their twin in this. The other conduit.

One male. One female. Both wearing the same expression of pain. Both hearing the same voice. Both bound to the same ritual. They shared the same hunger. The same desperation.

They touched the glass. Both reflections moved as one, separated by space but bound by blood and curse.

The voice inside pulsed, neither male nor female, something older that wore both like instruments.

Find the tether. Complete the circle. Or we burn from within.

The connection flickered. The second face faded. Only one remained, hollow-cheeked, desperate, no longer certain which impulses were their own.

They swallowed hard, pulled the hood lower, and vanished into the alley's shadows.

By the time the last note faded, the plaza was ordinary again. Sunlight. Footsteps.

CHAPTER 15

ERIK

$\mathcal{E}$rik had been keeping watch on Allie since she left her apartment.

From his truck across the street, he watched her collect coffee from the corner café. She paused at the courthouse steps before going inside. He told himself it was reconnaissance. Not obsession.

But when the air outside her building had shifted the night before and his scars had burned, he had known he could not simply watch any longer. Something in her was waking.

He parked two blocks from the courthouse, blended with the flow of suits and jurors, and found a seat at the back of her courtroom before the docket began. Close enough to feel the pull. Far enough not to draw attention.

When she entered, calm and collected, every nerve in his body responded. Heat stirred beneath his sleeve. His scars awakened, reaching toward her through the space between them.

Then she looked directly at him.

Green eyes. Storm green.

The air between them tightened. Not heat. Not fire. Recognition. His element reaching for hers. He tasted ozone. Felt pressure build behind his ribs.

Across the courtroom, Allie gasped. Her hand flew to her throat. The pendant beneath her blouse flared visible through the fabric, a pulse of blue light that beat in rhythm with his heart.

For one moment, she felt his heat and he felt her element. Not water. Something unruly. Storm-born.

Then Allie blinked, and the connection thinned, fading to a hum under his skin.

Erik's hands trembled. He gripped the bench until his knuckles whitened.

Bonds, once triggered, could not be undone. They could only be accepted or resisted.

He rose quietly and slipped out before she could look back. As he passed her row, his hand moved without thought. The card dropped from his palm, falling between the scattered notes on her table. She would find it. Or she would not. Either way, the choice would be hers.

Outside, sunlight struck him hard. He crossed to the plaza and bought coffee, something to hold while he waited.

From across the street, he watched her emerge onto the courthouse steps, briefcase clutched tight. She looked different. Tired. Pale. But not fragile. Something had shifted.

His fingers tightened around the cup. The bond hummed beneath his skin. Whatever line had once separated his world from hers was gone now.

He drained the coffee and tossed the cup. The fire in his veins still burned low and steady.

He slid behind the wheel of his truck. The thrum under his skin refused to fade.

He drove in silence. Turned onto a side street and parked behind a closed pawn shop.

He opened the glove box and pulled out a black folder. The Alliance emblem glinted in silver. Inside were reports from a closed case. *Mara Grayson.*

He had met her two years before the crash. The Alliance had flagged her as harmless. Low-level air dragon. He had wanted to believe it.

Now the case was stamped in red. Inactive. Subject deceased.

He turned the page. *Mara Grayson. Classification: Air Dragon.*

He stared at the classification line. If Allie carried storm, true storm, and they were sisters, then the Alliance had gotten Mara wrong. The pendant, if it had been suppressing power all along, dampening readings, the Alliance scanners would have missed it completely.

He scanned down. Guardianship, post-incident: *Eleanor Vance.*

His breath caught.

Vance was Watcher blood. Old line. Not Alliance-registered. Watchers did not take custody of dragonborn children without Council approval. They did not raise dragon girls in civilian homes. Unless they had been hiding them.

His hand tightened on the folder. If Eleanor Vance had raised both Grayson sisters, kept them off Alliance radar, suppressed their powers with artifacts, what had she been protecting them from?

He turned to the dependent line. *Dependent: Grayson, Alexandra.*

No classification. No elemental trace. Only name, age, and date of transfer.

This file was too clean. Someone had erased everything. As if both sisters had been buried.

He looked at the photo clipped inside. Two girls on a pier, wind in their hair. The older one wore a pendant, silver catching the sun.

He closed the folder slowly.

If he sent the report, the Alliance would come before he learned the truth. If he went in himself, he might not walk out.

He slipped the folder back into the glove box.

The Alliance would demand answers. But not yet. Not until he knew what she truly was.

He turned the ignition. The truck rumbled to life.

CHAPTER 16

ALLIE

*B*y the time she reached her apartment, the storm had not settled. The drive was a blur of lights and noise. She told herself sleep would fix everything. But when she closed the door behind her, the silence pressed in.

Allie stood in front of the bathroom mirror, hands braced on the sink.

Her eyes looked wrong. The green had always been dark, almost gray. Now they carried a rim of blue. Storm blue. Electric.

"You're imagining it," she told her reflection.

She turned on the faucet. Water rushed from the tap, and her breath caught. She could feel it. Not just see it. The flow carried weight, pressure, memory. Rain, river, ocean. The journey threaded through her mind without permission.

Her hands began to shake. "Stop. Stop."

She splashed her face. The cold shocked her back. When she looked up again, the water was only water. Her eyes were only eyes.

But her hands trembled. The pendant was warm. And somewhere deep in her chest, a whisper: You cannot fight what you are.

"I'm a lawyer," she said aloud, voice cracking. "I'm Allie Grayson.

I'm twenty-nine. I'm an ADA. I'm second chair on a fraud case." She swallowed. "I'm normal."

The pendant pulsed once. Thunder rumbled far off, though the sky outside was clear.

Allie sank to the bathroom floor, knees drawn to her chest. For the first time since the alley, she let herself admit the truth. Whatever normal had been, it was gone.

She stayed there until the tile pressed its chill through her skin and the shaking passed. Eventually, her breath slowed. That was enough.

She stood, dried her face, and moved to the living room. The pendant lay on the coffee table, pulsing in the lamplight. Beside it, Mara's photograph watched her.

Allie dropped onto the couch and pulled her laptop close. Her hands hovered above the keys. She was not sure what she meant to do. Instead, she stared at the search bar.

Glowing symbols in blood. Delete.

Storm hallucinations after trauma. Delete.

Finally, she typed: *Celtic sigil pendant prophecy.*

The results were mostly nonsense. Fantasy novels. New Age blogs. She was about to close the window when one link caught her eye. Scottish Folklore Archive. Digitized collection.

She clicked. The PDF loaded slowly. Columns of dense academic text. She scrolled without thinking, until a translated fragment stopped her cold.

When fire meets storm... six marks... the sleeping chain.

Her breath caught. She scrolled to the footnote. Elemental pairings. Binding curses. Pre-Christian traditions. Nothing concrete. Nothing real.

But the words vibrated through her chest.

She reached for the pendant. In the light, she saw it differently now. Tiny inscriptions shimmered along the edge. Marks she had never noticed before. They looked like the sigil from the alley, but gentler. Curved, not jagged.

Her eyes shifted to the photograph. "What were you wanting to tell me, Lena?"

The pendant pulsed. And for just a moment, Allie thought she heard her voice. Soft. Certain.

Find him.

CHAPTER 17

ERIK

*H*eat pulsed beneath Erik's skin, steady as a heartbeat. It had started minutes ago, unprovoked. He froze. The marks glimmered faintly, answering something distant.

Storm-light.

She was afraid. Not panicked, not screaming. Just afraid enough that the bond tugged at him like a thread pulled too tight. He felt the sharpness of it behind his ribs.

He closed his eyes and breathed slowly, pushing calm back along the connection. A quiet whisper of reassurance. The heat settled. Her fear eased, just slightly.

He opened his eyes and pulled his hand back from the window. The glass was warm where his palm had rested.

He turned to the map on his desk. Dallas sprawled beneath his hands. Four red marks dotted the city, each one linked by faded ink. Together they formed an unfinished circle.

He reached for the thin file marked *Case 0718-O* and flipped it open. The first photograph was grainy, washed out by flame.

Victim: *Milo Garran, forty-two, mechanic. Cause of death: smoke inhalation and severe burns.*

The photos showed what was left of the shop. Burned tools. Walls blackened in uneven crescents. The fire had started near the gas line, the investigation said, but the pattern was wrong. The marks curved inward, not outward.

He flipped to the autopsy summary. Deep laceration along the left abdomen. Pre-mortem bleed. Source unidentified.

The report called it debris trauma. Erik knew better. Someone had needed blood to draw with.

He sat back. Milo Garran. Earth dragon. Fire should not have taken him easily. Not without help. Not without intention.

He closed the file. He needed to see the place again.

He grabbed his coat and keys and stepped into the cooling night.

The drive to Oak Cliff took twenty minutes. He parked along the side lot where the chain-link fence sagged. The caution tape still clung to the posts, brittle from seven years of sun.

He pushed through and stepped into the ruins. The air was heavy with the memory of smoke, the scent clinging to brick and rust. The burn was too contained. The flame had curled inward, converging in a circular pattern.

He crouched near the workbench, brushing away soot until faint lines appeared. Etched into the concrete was a spiral, shallow and deliberate. The center was blackened deeper than the rest.

The scars along his arm responded instantly, glowing a muted red. The ground gave a low hum.

His fingers brushed the sigil, and heat flared up his arm. The scars ignited. The world tilted.

Recall came like a storm.

The ruin vanished. Milo Garran stood beneath a single lamp, humming as he worked. The forge breathed orange.

Then the air changed. In the far corner, a shadow moved. Someone kneeling, tracing a circle on the floor.

Milo turned. "Hey, you can't be here."

The figure looked up. The face was wrong, overlapping, male and female. The voice was calm. "Earth first."

The lamp flickered. The air snapped. Heat burst outward. The circle flared. The ground cracked. A beam fell.

The last thing Milo saw was the figure completing the circle, blood mixing with dust, as fire swallowed the room.

The vision tore apart.

Erik staggered back, breath ragged. The workshop was burned again. His nose was bleeding. His scars blazed white-hot. Too deep. The bond had dragged him farther than recall should reach.

He wiped the blood from his mouth and steadied his breath.

Recall always cost blood. Every dragon learned it early. Magic required sacrifice. The body paid what the mind demanded. Small workings drew sweat, pulled exhaustion from the bones. Larger spells required blood, nosebleeds, cuts that opened without warning, veins that burned beneath the skin. The greatest magics took pieces you never got back.

Erik had seen dragons hollow themselves out chasing power. He had watched them burn through their own reserves until nothing remained but ash and memory. The Alliance taught control for a reason. Magic answered need, but need had no mercy.

He steadied himself against the wall, the metallic taste still sharp on his tongue. The recall had shown him what he needed. The cost was worth it. She had been there. So the cost would always be worth it.

He stood and scanned the room again. The pattern was familiar, the same curvature from Mara's scene. The same deliberate symmetry.

His boot struck something that rang too clear. He crouched, brushing away ash until metal gleamed beneath. A medallion, blackened but intact.

He rubbed at the soot with his thumb. The fern pattern emerged. Beneath it, two letters: *M. G.*

Mara Grayson had been here. He felt it like a blow.

He waited for the hum, for recall. Nothing. The medallion was empty.

Still, the connection was too strong to ignore. The sigil's geometry matched the one from Mara's crash. Mara had been here. Not as a bystander. She had been looking for something. Investigating. Trying to stop something before it reached her.

The metal stayed warm in his palm, glimmering faintly when it caught the light. Stormlight.

He slipped the medallion into his pocket, jaw tight. The scars on his arm pulsed once, faint and steady.

He looked east toward the skyline. The horizon shimmered faint blue. He knew exactly where it came from.

Allie Grayson.

He turned back to the sigil, memorizing its size, its placement. Someone had known exactly what they were doing. The killer had started here with Earth.

He walked to his truck. The wind stirred through the wreckage, carrying the faint scent of ozone.

He started the engine and glanced at the map on the seat beside him. The inked circle had begun to make sense, its center resting near where the storm-light had risen.

The medallion sat on the passenger seat, its scorched edges catching the dying light.

Two more sites to check. Two more pieces of the pattern to confirm.

Behind him, the sigil flickered red once more, as if answering someone he could not yet see.

CHAPTER 18

ALLIE

The apartment held its breath. The words on the laptop screen refused to move.

When fire meets storm in children's grasp.

She closed the lid and let the quiet settle. It did not help.

Her phone lit with a calendar alert for a motions meeting at two. She stared at it until the screen dimmed. Work was a shelter, but not today.

She opened her work chat, typed *Personal emergency. I'll make up the review tomorrow,* and hit send before she could think twice.

Her thumb hovered over a name she had not called in months. The contact read simply: Aunt E. That was what she and Mara had always called Eleanor.

> Are you home this afternoon? I need to see you.

The typing dots appeared, disappeared, then returned.

> Always. Come by three. Bring tea if you remember which kind.

Allie crossed to the kitchen cabinet and pulled out the tin of bergamot tea. She measured two scoops into a small tin and tucked it into her purse. Then she grabbed her briefcase and turned to leave, then stopped. The second pendant still lay beside Mara's photograph. She slipped it into the felt pouch and tucked it into her briefcase's inner pocket.

By the time she reached the parking garage, the sky had shifted to a pale, uncertain blue. Traffic stitched itself along the highway. She merged and kept her eyes forward.

She took the Greenville exit and turned into a neighborhood where porches still held wind chimes. Eleanor's house waited beneath live oaks, white paint and stubborn roses.

The door opened before Allie could knock.

"You look like you slept beside a train," Eleanor said, voice dry. Her eyes, gray and sharp, moved immediately to Allie's throat where the pendant rested beneath her blouse. Something flickered there. Assessment, not concern.

"I didn't sleep much, Aunt E," Allie said.

Eleanor's smile faltered slightly. "Of course not. Lena was one of the bright ones." Then she nodded once. "Come in."

Allie stepped into the foyer and breathed in wood polish, bergamot, and old paper. She had been here dozens of times, but today the house felt smaller, the air close.

Eleanor touched her cheek briefly. Her eyes moved to the briefcase. "You brought it."

Allie lifted the travel tin. "Tea for my Aunt E."

Eleanor's expression softened. "Good girl." She set the kettle with a practiced hand.

They sat at the small table with sunlight filtering through lace. Steam rose between them. Eleanor poured, but her gaze kept returning to the thin outline of the pendant beneath Allie's blouse.

"Tell me what happened," Eleanor said.

Allie meant to hold back, but exhaustion loosened her tongue. She spoke of the alley, of Lena, of the mark that glowed, of the courtroom, of the water whispering.

Eleanor listened without interruption. When Allie finished, she set her cup down and reached out. "The pendant. May I?"

Allie hesitated. Some small instinct told her not to let go. But this was Aunt E. She pushed the unease aside and slid it forward.

Eleanor opened the pouch like a priest lifting a reliquary. The pendant lay in her palm, casting light along her fingers. She turned it over slowly, examining the markings. Her expression stayed neutral, but something behind her eyes flickered.

"I remember this pattern," she said at last. "Mara's pendant was nearly identical."

Eleanor's eyes lifted to Allie's throat, where the faint outline of another chain showed beneath her blouse.

"You brought me one," Eleanor said slowly. "But you're wearing another."

Allie's hand went to her chest. "Yes. This one is mine. The one you gave me at the funeral, from Mara."

Eleanor's expression shifted. "From Mara," she repeated softly. She looked down at the pendant in her palm, then back at Allie. "Are you certain which is which?"

Allie frowned. "Of course. I've been wearing mine for three years."

Eleanor said nothing. Her thumb brushed the pendant's edge, reverent and uncertain. This was the muting pendant. The one she had given Mara on her twelfth birthday.

Which meant the pendant around Allie's neck was something else entirely.

Eleanor's fingers tightened imperceptibly. "And when did the experiences begin? The sensations?"

"Yesterday morning. In the courthouse."

"Ah." Eleanor set the pendant down gently. "And the water, it spoke to you?"

"Yes. I could see where it had been."

Eleanor's cup rattled when she set it down. Her fingers froze mid-motion. For an instant, her mask slipped. "Storm tongue," she whispered.

"What?"

Her eyes snapped up, the word already swallowed. "No matter." Her voice lowered. "You were never meant to be caught in this."

The words landed heavy between them.

"Caught in what?"

Eleanor's hand closed over hers, the grip firmer than comfort. "Give it time, Allie. Some truths can't be rushed." But her eyes said something else entirely.

Eleanor crossed to the glass cabinet near the window. She unhooked the small brass key and fit it into the lock. The mechanism clicked softly. She drew out a single leather-bound book.

It looked older than the house itself, its spine cracked and the edges softened by decades of touch.

"This belonged to our ancestors," she said. "We pass it down when the changes begin."

"We?" Allie asked, a chill running along her spine.

"There are those of us who remember," Eleanor said. "Who watch the edges of the world."

"Watchers," Allie said slowly.

Eleanor's mouth curved. "An old name."

She set the book on the table. Allie stared at it, then reached toward it, almost out of defiance, but Eleanor's hand came down lightly over hers.

"Be careful," she said. "It remembers who opens it."

"What is it?"

"Records. Stories of our kind, written in a way that only those meant to understand can read."

Allie ran her fingers along the cover. The leather was cool at first, then warm, as if it recognized her touch. "You can read it?"

"Some of it. But the book chooses who it reveals itself to." Eleanor met her eyes. "And I think it's been waiting for you."

Allie's pulse quickened. "Why me?"

"Because you asked the right question." She did not say which one.

The book sat between them. When Allie brushed its spine, a pulse of warmth rose from her collarbone. Her pendant answered.

For an instant she saw something that was not the room at all, storm-light flashing over black water, wings rising through clouds. Then it was gone.

Her breath caught.

Eleanor's eyes flicked toward her. "Did you feel that?"

Allie nodded. "What was it?"

"An echo. A memory, perhaps." The curiosity in her tone was thinly veiled, but fear lingered underneath.

She drew the cabinet key back around her wrist. "Take the book. Read what you can. Come back tonight and tell me what it shows you."

Allie tucked the book into her briefcase. Her hand went to her throat. The pendant felt heavier than she remembered. Warmer.

"Bring the pendant too," Eleanor said, her tone light but not optional.

Allie paused at the door. For a moment she thought the house itself was listening. Then she nodded and left.

She stepped out into the afternoon. Above the oaks, clouds began to gather where the sky had been clear.

CHAPTER 19

ELEANOR

*E*leanor watched through the lace curtain until the car turned the corner.

When the headlights disappeared, she remained at the window as the rain began. She pressed her fingers to the glass and whispered a quiet prayer. Protection always came with a price. She only hoped Allie would survive hers.

Only then did she reach into her pocket for the phone she never saved numbers in.

The line rang once before a voice answered.

"It's confirmed," she said. "She's manifesting. Storm aligned. Stronger than Mara."

A beat of silence followed.

"Yes. She has a pendant. Two, actually."

Another pause. Eleanor's fingers tightened around the phone.

"No, she doesn't know yet. But she will."

Silence stretched. When she spoke again, her voice had softened.

"I need you. And I think, deep down, you still need her."

The silence cracked. Soft breath. No words.

"I wouldn't ask if there were another way. They told me to report immediately. Or they'll come. No warnings. No second chances."

She could still hear the cold finality in that Watcher's voice years ago.

We erase liabilities. We don't bury the dead.

"You saved them once," she said. "You stopped them. The night the house burned. You brought them to me before the Watchers could finish what they started. You gave them a chance."

A sound crackled over the line. Pain. Memory.

"She'll be here tonight. Eight o'clock. She trusts me. Come before they do."

Her voice hardened. "No shadows. No death sentence."

Another breath.

"I gave her the book. She won't stay in the dark for long."

She closed her eyes. "Please."

She ended the call and looked down at the faint shimmer of blue light bleeding through the table's wood.

Fourteen years earlier, she had made another call. A hedge witch in Galveston who dealt in bindings and silence. Three weeks later a package arrived. Inside were two pendants wrapped in black silk. The note had read: One to mute. One to guide. Choose carefully.

She had given Mara the muting pendant on her twelfth birthday. For six years, it worked. Mara grew up quiet. Safe. Normal.

Then she turned eighteen and began asking questions. About the fire. About her parents' deaths. About the pressure beneath her skin.

Eleanor should have told her then. Instead, she had lied.

And Mara had believed her. Right up until the night she did not.

Eleanor crossed to the glass cabinet and took out a small wooden box she had not touched in years. Inside, wrapped in black silk, lay the second pendant, the guiding pendant.

Which meant whatever Allie was wearing, whatever was amplifying her power, had come from somewhere else.

The witch had said the guiding pendant would help the bearer understand their power. It was meant for the moment after the muting pendant came off.

But Mara had never received it. Eleanor had been too afraid.

Now Allie was manifesting without guidance, moving through

power she did not understand, wearing a pendant Eleanor had never seen before.

She did not know what that meant. Not yet.

Eleanor closed the box and returned it to the cabinet, locking it with a quiet click.

"I'm sorry, child," she whispered to the empty room. "You were never meant to wake this way."

Outside, the wind chime stirred once. Thunder answered.

She picked up her phone and typed a message:

> She'll be here at 8 p.m. Come alone. She trusts me.

She hit send before she could change her mind.

Her ally would arrive first. Between them, they might be able to negotiate. Contain this. Keep Allie from the fate that had taken others before her.

Or they would all burn together.

Outside, thunder moved closer.

CHAPTER 20

KILLER

Inside the old warehouse, the first killer knelt in the circle's center. The sigil pulsed faintly beneath their knees. The blade opened their palm. Blood slid into the carved lines. Light spread outward, then dimmed.

Complete.

Then another pulse rose through the silence. Not theirs. A second mind tethered to the same call.

The second of them stood on the roof of a parking garage near Love Field. Wind pressed against their coat. The pulse told them enough. The circle was sealed. The next rhythm had begun.

They waited in shadow as the door opened. A man stepped out, pulling his jacket tighter. The sky above him moved in patterns only he could read, aircraft descending through clouds. He breathed deeply, unaware he had already been chosen.

The observer watched. The movement of his hands as he gestured to the sky. Tracing invisible paths through the air. The wind followed him, responding to something in his blood he had never named.

When the man turned back inside, the observer smiled. The control tower glowed against the dark. The next element would not be gentle.

In the warehouse, the first figure closed the circle with a slow breath. The blue light dimmed.

"It begins again," they said.

Across the city, the other felt the words pass through them. Together, miles apart, they moved in the same rhythm. One finished what the other began.

At Love Field, the man returned to his station, headset crackling. Tomorrow he would guide planes as he had for twelve years. Tomorrow the air would answer a voice that was not his own.

One remained. The fourth sigil, carved into the alley wall behind the bar. Its pattern was fractured. It needed to be fixed. A small sacrifice. Blood to complete the pattern.

The observer turned from the roof, already walking. The ritual would hold. The city would bend. Air would answer.

Air would be the next. And when it fell, the circle would nearly close. Two more elements. Two more lives. Then the chain would wake.

CHAPTER 21

ALLIE

The afternoon had faded outside Eleanor's cottage. Wind chimes stirred once as Allie reached the car.

She drove without turning on the radio. Dallas at dusk blurred past the windows. Her mind replayed Eleanor's warning, the strange pull when the pendant met the old book.

She should go home. She should read Eleanor's book.

But her hands turned the wheel east instead of north. Toward Deep Ellum. Toward the Black Cat.

The streets were nearly empty. She parked beside the darkened bar. Police tape fluttered in the alley.

The door bore a city seal sticker. Clearance pending. The lock turned easily. She stepped inside and locked the door behind her.

The smell hit her first: stale beer, cleaner, and beneath it the faint ghost of blood. The fluorescents buzzed to life.

She moved behind the bar, hands brushing the familiar wood. Nothing unusual until she crouched to check the bottom cabinet, the one Lena always kept locked. New hardware.

She tried her keys. None fit.

"Key," she muttered. "You said key. Where..."

The pendant pulsed, then pulled toward the office.

Allie followed.

The small room smelled of cigarettes and vanilla. Her fingers brushed the wall behind the desk. The wallpaper felt wrong. She pressed harder. A hidden panel clicked open.

Inside waited a metal box and a folded sheet of paper. The name Lena was written across the top in Mara's handwriting.

The air seemed to thin. She sank into the chair and unfolded the note.

Hey Lena,
If I don't make it back, this box is for Allie.
Inside are things she'll need.
The pendant with it's not the old one Aunt E gave me.
It's mine. Keep it safe and give it to her if something happens to me.
Take care of her for me.
Mara

The note trembled in Allie's hands. She set it aside and reached for the box.

The keyhole was small. When she tilted it toward the light, she saw a faint symbol etched around the rim. It looked like the outline of the pendant.

She reached into her coat pocket and pulled Lena's pendant from the pouch. The metal was cool as she held it near the box. Nothing happened.

She set it on the desk and looked down at the pendant she had worn since Mara died. Its stone glowed faintly, a soft blue pulse.

Slowly, she unclasped the chain and held it in her hand. The metal was warm. She laid it beside Lena's.

The one she had worn was brighter, newer, its etchings sharp. The one from the pouch was darker, tarnished, the engravings softened by time.

She turned them over. The tarnished one carried tiny lettering: *MG*. Mara Grayson.

The other was unmarked, its silver clean, newer.

She stared at them, memory slipping back to the funeral. Eleanor's hand closing over hers. Mara would want you to have this.

She had worn it for three years, right up until two nights ago. She must have accidentally swapped them, clasped the wrong one in the dark.

The one she had been wearing had been Lena's. That was why the courthouse had tilted. Why the water had whispered.

But even as the thought formed, she felt the lie in it. The pendant had been the key. But the power had come from her. From her blood. Waiting.

And now it was awake.

She lifted the unmarked pendant and held it to the lock. The glow deepened. Light threaded through the box's etchings. A low hum filled the air. The mechanism released with a quiet metallic sigh.

The box opened.

Inside lay a leather journal, worn soft. Mara's handwriting filled the first page. Beneath it were photographs and files. At the bottom, a manila folder: *GRAYSON FIRE, APRIL 2006*.

Her parents. She opened it. The official report: electrical fault, case closed. Clipped to it was a photograph of her childhood home reduced to ash. On the walkway, faint but visible, a sigil. The same pattern from the alley wall.

Her knees gave way. She sank to the floor, staring at the photograph. When she could breathe again, she reached for the journal.

She opened it. Her thumb ran along the first line.

March 12

The storm tonight felt wrong. The pendant went cold, then hot. The fire that killed Mom and Dad wasn't an accident. I remember a mark on the ground.

She turned pages faster.

April 28

I took off Aunt E's pendant and left it next to Dad's pen. When I woke, Dad's pen was gone and a pendant was next to mine. Identical but alive. When I wore it, I felt whole.

September 8

We're close. The sigils aren't random. They're building a circle.

September 12

This may be my last entry. I gave Lena the pendant and box. If you are reading this, Allie, I'm sorry. We were supposed to die with Mom and Dad. Someone wants to finish it. Be careful who you trust. Even Aunt E. I love you.

The journal ended there. Three days later, Mara had died.

Allie sat surrounded by ghosts. The journal, the files, the photograph. Proof that everything she had believed was a lie.

She noticed something beneath the journal. She brushed papers aside. A brooch lay inside, wrapped in black silk. Old silver, its clasp worn smooth. At the center rested a scale, silvery white, translucent.

The moment she touched it, warmth flooded her fingers. The room vanished.

Cold air filled her lungs. Snow drifted from a pewter sky. A young woman stood ahead, wrapped in furs. Serena. In a hollow of snow lay a dragon, silver scales dulled by frost, blood darkening the ground. An arrow jutted from its wing. Serena knelt.

"Because you are alive," she whispered. "And that should mean something."

She pulled the arrow free. Light erupted, silver and blue. The wound sealed. A single scale fell into the snow. The dragon exhaled.

For my lifeblood spared, may its memory never fade.

The vision shattered.

Allie gasped, the office slamming back. She was on her knees, one hand braced against the wood, the other clutching the brooch.

The air smelled faintly of pine.

She stood, wiping her face. The brooch was warm in her palm.

Thunder rolled far off. The fluorescents hummed a single note and fell quiet.

A floorboard creaked. Allie froze. The front door. She had locked it.

The lock turned without a hand touching it. The door eased inward. A faint current moved through the bar, carrying the scent of rain.

Someone was inside. Allie clutched the box to her chest, the pendant burning hot against her skin.

The lights flickered once, then steadied. The office door began to open.

And the storm moved with it.

CHAPTER 22

ERIK

The memorial cross waited near the guardrail by White Rock Lake. Silk flowers sagged under weather. Three years since the crash.

Erik reached for the case file on the passenger seat. Mara Grayson, single-vehicle collision. Fatal injuries.

He flipped to the autopsy page. Severe laceration to the left flank, depth exceeding expected range for crash trauma. Cause of death: *exsanguination.*

Wounds too deep. Blood loss too rapid. And the timing matched the ritual killings.

He followed a trail of scorched grass down the hill, blackened stems leading from the guardrail to the waterline. No fire reported at the scene. Just rain, impact, and death.

He returned to the guardrail. He pulled the medallion from his pocket and held it. His scars began to heat.

He pressed his palm to the rail, closed his eyes, and let the recall take him.

He was Mara. Terrified. Running. Hands gripping the wheel. Rain hammered the windshield. Lightning cracked. Someone else was on the road. She pressed the accelerator. The curve tightened. Tires caught water. The car skidded. Metal screamed. Impact. Glass shattered. Rain poured through the broken window.

Then a shadow moved outside. Not the Watchers. Someone else. Hooded. The figure crouched beside the window and raised a knife. The blade slid into Mara's side with calm precision. Blood welling fast.

A voice whispered, soft and wrong, layered. "Three marks complete. Three remain. The vessel will open. The storm born will burn."

The figure traced something on the guardrail. A spiral. Glowing red.

The last thing she saw was the sigil burning brighter.

Erik staggered back, chest heaving. Blood ran from his nose. His scars burned white-hot. But he did not fall this time.

Something had changed. A warmth moved through him, foreign yet familiar. Storm energy. Not his. Borrowed.

The bond.

He wiped the blood away and stared at the guardrail.

The realization hit him. He had felt Allie's power through the bond. Storm. Not fire. Not earth. Storm.

His mind raced. Mara Grayson, classified as air-born three years ago. But if Allie was storm-born, and they were sisters...

"Shit," he breathed.

The Alliance had gotten it wrong. Sisters shared bloodlines. If Allie carried storm, then Mara had too.

Which meant the second mark had been storm. Not air.

He pulled out his notebook with shaking hands and drew a hard line through "Air" next to Mara's name. Above it he wrote:

STORM.

Earth. Storm. Fire. Water. That left Air and Spirit.

The killer's words echoed: The storm born will burn.

Not Mara in the past tense. Allie. Now.

The ritual was accelerating. And Allie was the next target.

He pulled out his phone. He typed.

Pretty sure Mara Grayson was murdered.

The reply came fast.

Can you prove it?

The recall showed a stabbing after the crash.

That's not proof.

Working on it.

Don't do anything stupid.

Erik pocketed the phone. He turned back to the rail, rain running off his sleeve.

* * *

THE WATER TREATMENT plant sat at the edge of the city, half buried under fog and floodlights. Erik parked behind abandoned utility trucks. The pull in his chest had led him here.

Carlos Mendez. Fire dragon. Found deceased three weeks ago. Cause: *heatstroke.*

He stepped through the breach in the fence. The pump house loomed ahead. He moved along the walkway until he found the police sticker on Building C.

The panel outside Server Room B read eighty-seven degrees. The vents were frosted over, ice choking airflow. The system was fighting itself.

Erik pushed the door open. Dry, heavy heat.

Yellow tape sagged across the doorway. He stepped inside.

The floor around the chalk outline was bone dry. Concrete cracked in a spiderweb pattern, radiating from where Carlos had fallen. The edges were glassy.

Carlos had been fire-born. His body ran hot, but not this hot. Not enough to crack concrete. Unless someone had pulled the water out of him.

"Heatstroke," Erik said quietly. "Right."

He crouched. Crystals lined the grooves, too uniform. When he pressed his thumb against them, they melted instantly. Condensation formed again almost immediately.

He pulled out his scanner. No accelerant. But there was an electromagnetic reading, faint and rhythmic.

He swept his light across the servers. On the side panel, something caught the beam.

A sigil. Small, precise, drawn in crystalline powder.

The spiral pattern was identical to the others.

It was not salt. It was Carlos. The water drawn from his body, crystallized and used to seal the mark that killed him.

Erik's stomach tightened. The killer had made him part of the ritual.

He reached out. The air shimmered faintly. It bit through the leather, sharp. The vibration was pressure, dense and crushing.

He jerked his hand back. The glove was wet. The moisture had come from him.

It had taken the water from him.

"Hydro extraction," he said softly. "That's not human work."

"You always did ignore warnings," a voice said behind him.

He did not turn immediately. "Kael. You stalking me now?"

Kael leaned against the desk, saxophone case slung over one shoulder. She wore the same leather jacket, weathered at the elbows.

"You were at the bar last night and courthouse today," Erik said.

She nodded once. "You've got a habit of walking through my songs."

"I've a habit of doing my job."

Kael's eyes flicked to his notebook. "That mark isn't finished. Whoever made it doesn't understand what they're stirring." She hesitated. "There are patterns older than the Alliance. The kind that wake things better left buried."

Erik waited. "You know what it is?"

"I think so," she said. "But saying its name might call it faster."

He studied her. Kael had always been like smoke. Once an informant, sometimes an ally, always dangerous.

"I'm sorry about Mara."

Her expression softened. A little.

She crossed her arms. "This sigil is still feeding."

"I noticed." He nodded toward it. "You see the residue?"

"I see what's left of him," she said. "Carlos called me. Said someone was watching the plant. Someone wrong."

"Did he see them?"

"Shadows. After dark. I told him to report it. He didn't get the chance."

Erik's jaw tightened. "You trusted the Alliance?"

"I trusted they'd ignore it. Like they did with Mara."

The accusation sat between them.

"I'm here now," Erik said.

"Too late."

The mist thickened. The sigil pulsed beneath their feet.

"This was ritual," Erik said. "Deliberate."

Kael nodded. "And it's learning."

"I think they're building elemental balance. Fire, earth, storm, water."

"It doesn't feel like one hand," she said. "More like two voices drawing the same shape."

Erik went still. "Two killers?"

"Two conduits. Feeding the same source."

"What's controlling them?"

"I don't know. But it's old."

He rose. "What do you know?"

"The marks are calling something back. And she's caught in it. The woman with the storm in her eyes."

Erik saw Allie's face again. "Say it clearly."

Kael stepped closer. "The bond won't protect her. It'll expose her. Every Watcher will see."

Before he could speak, she stepped into the mist. "Be careful where you draw your lines, Fire Born. In the end, everybody burns."

Then she was gone.

Erik stood motionless, her words lingering like a curse.

He closed his notebook and walked back to his truck.

Behind him, the fog rippled once.

Pressure built behind his eyes, sudden and brutal. The ground vibrated. He staggered forward, catching himself on the truck. The air above shimmered bright blue.

The hum from the sigil moved beneath his skin.

A surge struck, dragging him down through the connection.

Then silence.

When he came to, he was on the ground. The air hung heavy with burnt ozone.

His scars burned differently now. Not draining. Feeding. The bond thrummed beneath his ribs, pulling energy from somewhere east.

Pulling from her.

He had survived by pulling from her. The bond had saved him before either of them understood what it could do.

Another heartbeat moved inside his.

Light against flame. Pulling east. Storm-light. Allie.

The curse was moving. And she was its next point.

He pushed to his feet and staggered toward the truck. He slid into the driver's seat and started the engine.

The bond burned steady beneath his skin. A heartbeat that was not his.

Leading him toward the storm. Toward her.

CHAPTER 23

KILLER

The hum of the servers was gone. Only the quiet drip of condensation remained.

A figure stood where Erik had knelt, the glow from their gloves pale in the dark. The sigil was dead, but not cold. It still held power.

They traced a finger through the residue, gathering white dust, and rubbed it between their fingers. The texture was right. The pattern was wrong.

Someone had interfered.

"Impatient," they murmured.

This was not their sigil. It was the other one's work. The second conduit. They had drawn the circle, but the lines were heavy with something colder than blood. Death magic. The kind that fed fast but demanded its price later.

They touched the residue again. The air stung their fingertips.

The other heartbeat was distant. The rhythm that had moved with theirs for weeks was silent.

They knelt and brushed away the edge of the spiral, exposing the melted concrete beneath. Blue light glimmered faintly.

"Still hungry," they said softly.

From a pocket came a sliver of crystal. They touched it to the mark, and the line brightened, feeding for an instant before fading again.

Not enough. The resonance was broken. The pattern needed balance. Two hands. Two voices.

They rose and turned toward the door. As they passed the body outline, the air cooled. A faint shimmer of salt lifted to follow, clinging to their sleeve.

Outside, lightning split the sky.

They stood in the rain, head tilted, listening. Beneath the thunder and the steady hiss of water, another sound emerged. A heartbeat, distant and rhythmic, pulsing from somewhere far east.

Their smile deepened.

"Found you," they said.

Then they turned toward the highway and followed the pulse into the dark.

CHAPTER 24

ERIK

The rain chased him from White Rock Lake to Deep Ellum. Dallas glowed ahead, the skyline half-buried in mist.

He parked near Elm Street and killed the engine. His head still throbbed from the recall. The medallion in his pocket had gone silent, but the silence was not peace.

He crossed into the alley behind the Black Cat. It looked clean under the streetlights, but death left stains no soap could reach.

Erik stood in the center. The sigil had been washed away, yet his scars still answered its ghost. Heat stirred under his skin. Water. The fourth element. The fourth death.

He crouched and pressed his palm to the brick. Cold stone. Cold blood. But beneath it, something still moved.

The air shifted, charged.

"You feel it too."

The voice came from the mouth of the alley. A woman stepped into the light, curled hair catching rain, eyes flickering gold, a saxophone case slung over one shoulder.

"Air-born," Erik said quietly.

She stepped closer. "You found Mara's medallion."

His hand moved to his pocket. He drew the medallion out slowly.

"I put it back when I realized you were heading there," Kael said. "Thought you might be able to get something from it."

He turned the medallion in his hand. "It needs a home," he said, extending it.

Kael studied him before reaching out. Her fingers curled around the metal. "I will keep it for now. Allie might want it back."

Erik nodded once.

Something shifted across Kael's face. The wind changed between them, colder.

"You saw what happened at the lake," she said. "You saw her die."

Erik's jaw tightened. "I saw it. The crash. The blood."

Kael closed her eyes. "Then you know."

For a moment, he said nothing. The rain filled the silence.

"I've spent every night since tracking this killer," Kael said. "Following the pattern. And now you show up thinking you can just solve it?"

Erik opened his mouth, but the word *pattern* snagged something deep in his memory.

"It might be the old Morna myth," Kael said, her voice dropping low. "The pattern lines up."

Erik froze. Morna. The witch who had cursed them all. A bedtime story, until the Alliance made him a hunter.

"She did not just curse us," Kael said. "She bound us. The sigils are recharging it."

Erik's stomach dropped. "The Alliance knows."

"Of course they do. They just do not talk about it."

"Then we take this to them."

"And tell them what? They would pull Allie in and cut her open before asking questions."

"Not all of them are like that."

"Name one."

"Torvald."

Kael's expression flickered. "Your handler."

"My mentor. There is a difference."

"Is there?" But she did not push.

"If we show him what we have," Erik said, "he might help."

"And if he does not? If they decide Allie is a risk?"

"Then we move first," Erik said. "We protect her."

Kael exhaled. "Then we keep digging."

She looked past him toward the bar. The wind rose around her, colder now.

"Then tell me what I do not know," Erik said.

"There was mention of a vessel," Kael said. "Something meant to contain the awakening. But the texts were not clear."

"The vessel," he said quietly. His mind leapt to Allie.

Kael's gaze sharpened. "You've met her."

"Briefly."

"Then stay away from her."

"It is too late," Erik said. "The bond is already forming."

Kael went still. "You are serious."

He nodded once. "It happened in the courthouse. Fire and storm recognized each other."

Kael's voice dropped to a whisper. "She is wearing Mara's pendant."

Erik nodded.

Kael's eyes darkened. "Then she dies like Mara."

Erik leaned against the wall. "We do not know enough. This could be ritual. Could be personal."

"Too clean for that. Too precise."

"Still does not mean it is the curse."

"No," she said. "But it feels like it."

Kael turned toward the mouth of the alley.

"Wait," Erik said. "If we cannot stop it before the sixth mark, we will not stop it at all."

"I know."

"Then we start with the fifth."

"You know who it is?"

"Air-born," Erik said. "Marcus Thorne. Air traffic controller. Love Field Airport."

Kael's eyes widened. "How do you know?"

"The medallion showed me fragments."

"Then we are already late."

They walked out together, rain smearing the lights. The wind flared, scattering debris. Kael turned her face toward it, eyes closing.

"She is moving," she whispered. "The storm-born. She went back to the bar."

Erik felt it too, a ripple of power, faint but growing.

Another flash split the sky. For a heartbeat, the faded sigil on the wall glowed red, its pattern shining through the water.

Erik froze. Heat surged beneath his skin. The mark pulsed once, alive, before fading.

He staggered, bracing against the wall as the scars along his forearm blazed, veins of gold pulsing beneath the skin.

Kael turned toward him. "You felt that too."

The sigil ignited again, fierce. The brick burned white hot, lines flaring like a waking eye. The light threw their shadows long, then vanished.

"She is inside," Erik said, voice strained. "That came from her."

Kael's eyes widened. "That was not a surge."

"She just opened something."

They both turned toward the back door of the bar, the rain swallowing their footsteps as thunder rolled closer.

CHAPTER 25

KILLER

*B*eyond the rain hitting the abandoned café window, the Black Cat sat dark and silent.

They pressed a palm to the cold pane. The air shimmered faintly. A small working, just enough to mask their presence. Not enough to stop what was coming.

Across the street, in the alley behind the bar, two figures moved through the rain. One fire. One air. Hunters. Investigators. Too late to stop anything.

The fire-born carried heat beneath his skin, scars glowing faintly even through fabric. The air-born moved like wind, restless and searching. Neither looked toward the café. The working held.

Inside the bar, another presence stirred. Not the investigators. Not the girl. The second conduit. Preparing. Moving through the space with purpose.

They felt it through the connection. A distant warmth. A rhythm not their own. The mark on their wrist pulsed once, answering.

The network waited beneath the city. Four marks glowing faint and steady. Three complete. One broken. The broken one sat inside the bar, fractured but not dead. It could still be used. Would be used.

Two more after this, and the pattern would hold.

They lifted their hand again to the window, watching the alley. The fire-born staggered suddenly, bracing against the wall. The air-born turned toward him, alarmed.

Good. They felt it. The surge from inside.

The sacrifice had died. The sigil was repaired. Everything was moving as it should.

Across the street, red light flickered in the bar windows. Brief. Bright. Gone.

The ritual could continue.

They removed their hand from the glass and rose. Time to move. The fifth mark waited at Love Field, unaware. Air would fall next. Then the vessel would be needed, and the chain would wake.

They pulled their coat tight and turned toward the door, waiting for confirmation.

But before they could move, the air went still.

And the ground came up to kiss their face.

CHAPTER 26

ALLIE

Thunder rolled low. The office lights flickered once, then steadied. A metallic click followed as the front lock turned.

Her breath sharpened. She held the box tight against her chest. The brooch burned in her pocket. No one should have had a key.

She reached for the lamp, turned it off, and slipped toward the back wall. The pendant at her throat pulsed once, cold and sharp.

The front door opened. A silhouette stepped inside, shoulders broad beneath a heavy coat. A flashlight beam swept across the floor.

Detective Hargrove.

What was he doing here? She had seen him at the courthouse hours ago. He had handled Lena's case. Called it a robbery.

She slipped behind the office door, back pressed to the wall. The pendant flared again. Instinct took over. The air shifted. Sound dulled. Her breath vanished into the hum of rain. She felt herself fade from sight.

A calm settled over her. She did not understand it, but she stayed still.

He crossed the room and closed the door with care. Moved to the desk. Put on gloves. Drew a small photograph of Lena from the drawer. Then a glass vial filled with something red and faintly luminous.

Allie's fingers brushed the pendant. It warmed in warning.

He added a small leather pouch. It twitched once. He hesitated, checked his phone, jaw tightening.

"No need," he muttered. "The sigil's still charging."

He pocketed the phone and left the pouch unopened. Uncorked the vial. Let one drop fall onto the desk. It hissed. A faint spiral spread through the wood, glowing red. The same sigil from the alley.

He pressed his palms flat to the mark and began to speak.

"The fourth is sealed. The fifth awaits. Blood calls to blood. Fire calls to..."

The pattern stuttered. Something was pulling at it, unraveling the edges. Light erupted.

Hargrove's eyes snapped open. "What..."

The sigil latched onto him. His skin blistered. He tried to pull back, but his hands fused to the desk.

"No. Elena..." he whispered.

The desk hissed. The mark blazed white-hot. Smoke curled from his sleeves.

"She lied," he said, bitter.

Then his eyes found her. Even through the shimmer, he saw.

"The storm girl," he rasped. "The vessel. Elena wins."

Allie's blood went cold. Elena. Who was Elena?

The sigil flared. His next breath turned to smoke.

Then he was gone. Melted into the ground right before her.

The glow collapsed inward. No body remained, only the spiral burned into the floor, pulsing once, twice. The light did not die. It spread.

Threads of crimson crawled across the floor toward the walls. Where they touched shadow, they vanished.

Allie felt it through the pendant. A pulse racing outward, crossing miles. She pressed a trembling hand to her chest.

The pendant pulsed, too bright to look at. Heat surged behind her eyes. Not fire, but pressure. The air shuddered.

The sigil convulsed. Sound vanished. The pull dragged at her bones.

The magic imploded.

The light folded inward, drawn through her like a reversed breath. The pendant drank it in. Her body lifted from the floor.

For one heartbeat, she saw everything. The city's lines of power. The sigils like stars. Erik's fire in motion. Wild wind surrounding a woman she had never seen before, moving with him.

Then the vision shattered.

Thunder cracked. The sigil vanished. Ash blew outward. The pendant dimmed.

But the energy did not leave her. It surged inward, settling into the rhythm of her heart.

The world tilted. Allie reached for the desk. Missed. The floor rose to meet her.

White. Then black.

CHAPTER 27

ERIK

The alley behind the Black Cat erupted in light. Erik stumbled as the faded sigil on the wall flared crimson. The air shook.

Kael threw up an arm. "What the hell was that?"

Before he could answer, the atmosphere shifted. A ripple rolled through the alley, warm and sharp. His breath caught. The marks on his arm pulsed bright.

"You feel that?"

Kael nodded, gold flaring in her eyes. "Big magic. It's coming from inside."

Another ripple struck. The lights above the door blew out. Silence followed, thick and unnatural, folding inward.

Erik moved toward the door. Kael caught his arm. "There's a veil. Someone sealed this place."

A third surge hit. The brick behind them glowed red. The shock-wave struck.

Erik slammed into the wall. Kael dropped to one knee, wind spiraling around her.

Then came the scream. Not human. It rose from inside the building and echoed inside their bones.

Erik pushed to his feet. His scars blazed. "Now."

Kael stepped forward, whispering. The air rippled outward. The door trembled. Wind folded into the lock.

Erik threw his shoulder against it, fire flaring through the frame. The latch snapped. The door blasted open.

The hallway beyond was dark. Every bulb had shattered. The air reeked of smoke and ozone.

The barroom lay in ruin. Tables overturned. Bottles shattered. The piano split down the middle.

Erik pressed forward, drawn toward the office. The door was warped. The handle was half-melted.

"She's in there," he said.

He reached for the handle. Metal scorched his palm, but he turned it. The latch gave. The door groaned open.

Cold air spilled out. Then the pressure broke.

Wind burst past them. The office was wrecked. The desk had split in two, one half scorched, the other slick with melted varnish. A faint spiral carved into the wood pulsed red, then dimmed.

Allie lay curled in the corner, her arms locked around a scorched metal box. The pendant at her throat glowed faintly.

Erik dropped beside her. "She's breathing."

Kael knelt. "What happened?"

Erik reached toward her. The pendant sparked. A lash of light sliced across his hand. He hissed.

"It's protecting her," Kael said.

Allie's breath hitched. Her back arched.

Erik touched her arm. The pendant pulsed, then dimmed under his hand. Her eyes fluttered.

"Who..."

"You're safe," Erik said.

Her hand found his. Fingers curled weakly around his wrist.

The bond caught.

Light snapped between them, silver and gold, fire and storm. Her pulse struck his like a second heartbeat.

For an instant, she was awake. Then the light vanished. She went still.

The bond ignited. A blinding pulse tore through him. His scars flared molten. The world tilted.

He saw her light, a thread running from her heart to his. It pulsed once, twice, then locked in place.

Fire to storm. Her pulse aligned with his. He pulled back, desperate to sever it, but the thread held.

He broke contact. The pulse receded, but the connection remained.

Kael gripped his shoulder. "Erik."

He turned. His eyes were wild.

"You bonded," she said quietly.

"It was not…" He looked away. "She doesn't even know."

Thunder cracked outside. Kael rose, wind coiling around her. She pressed a hand to Allie's chest. Air stirred, wrapping around her breath.

Allie's breathing steadied.

"She stable?" Erik asked.

Kael nodded. "For now. But this woke something."

Erik stared at the smoldering sigil. "Then we get her out."

He lifted Allie into his arms. The pendant pressed against his chest, pulsing in rhythm with his own.

Kael opened the door and looked back once. The sigil had cooled, but the air still tasted of iron.

Rain poured in, cool and cleansing.

Far across the skyline, in a windowless room lit by a single candle, another sigil stirred.

CHAPTER 28

ELENA

*R*ed light burst across the stone. The fire veined outward, uncontrolled, hissing toward the outer ring.

The woman flinched back, hand singed, breath caught. The sigil pulsed once. Then it cracked. A fracture split the outer glyph, and the light dimmed, choking.

Smoke curled from the edge of the vessel. The candle guttered.

"No, no, no."

She dropped to her knees beside the mark, fingers skimming the charred circle. Heat licked at her palm. The core was still alive. Barely. A single line remained intact, faintly glowing.

She pressed trembling fingers to the sigil, and for a moment, fire flickered beneath her skin. Old water. Dragon water from a line that predated the Alliance itself.

"Come on," she whispered. "Hold, damn you."

The vessel did not answer.

She pressed a crystal shard to the center. Nothing.

Again. Still nothing.

Then a flicker. A slow pulse.

She exhaled, chest shaking. Relief and fury.

"Too close," she muttered. "Too soon. I promised it would work. I promised."

She stared down at the damage. The vessel was not gone. But it was no longer whole. Something in the sigil had buckled. She did not know if it could be rebuilt.

The storm overhead growled, and the candle flared back to life. The mark throbbed once more.

Not dead. Not yet.

She sank back on her heels. "We can still begin," she said softly.

But there was no triumph in her voice now.

She rose, wiping ash from her hands.

"Forgive me," she whispered to the empty room. "Forgive me, mi hijo."

She pressed her hand to her chest, where the bond had been. Where Jacob's fire had lived until the curse tore him from her. Morna had promised. When the sixth mark burned, when the vessel opened, the bond would restore. She had sacrificed her son for that promise.

Outside, thunder cracked. And beneath the city, something turned in its sleep.

CHAPTER 29

KILLER

across the street, in the ruins of a forgotten café, another circle burned.

The light hit her before the sound. One moment she was at the window, the sigil in her palm glowing steady. The next, the world cracked open.

Magic screamed through the air. The circle collapsed. The power snapped back, wild and wrong.

The blast hurled her against the far wall. Glass erupted around her. Her breath left in a single sound.

She lay still, stunned. Her fingers twitched toward the tether stone meant to seal the fourth sigil. Cracked. Burned through.

No.

This was not how it was meant to go.

Four sigils. Earth. Storm. Fire. Water. Each one marked. But something had broken the pattern.

She forced herself upright. Pain bloomed behind her ribs. Her magic sputtered. She pressed her hand to her side, where the sigil was etched in her skin. The lines had blackened, some burned away entirely.

Across the street, the Black Cat glowed. Storm-light pulsed

through wood and stone. The curse still moved. But not toward her. Not toward the gate. It had gone to the girl.

She dragged herself forward. Something had awakened, but it was not what they had summoned.

This was not a failed ritual. This was a theft.

Then she saw them, the vessel, the fire-born, and the air-born.

They burst from the bar, and she knew. The vessel had taken the charge.

Through the rain, she saw it, a golden thread pulsing from the shattered circle to the girl in the truck.

Her voice shook. "You were not meant to be there."

She looked down at her palm. Blood and glass.

She had been meant to be the gate. Elena had promised it. Had trained her to hold that power.

But the spell had chosen another.

She staggered to her feet. Each step left blood behind. The sigil on her arm flickered once, then guttered out.

She would have to rebuild. Find Elena. Understand why the curse had turned from her.

The fourth sigil was broken, not fulfilled.

And if the spell no longer recognized her as its gate, then she would burn whatever it did choose.

Vessel or not.

She did not look back.

CHAPTER 30

ERIK

*R*ain came down in cold sheets the moment they stepped outside. The alley that had shimmered minutes ago was now only water.

Erik adjusted Allie's weight in his arms, careful not to jar her. She was still clutching the box, her fingers locked tight. The pendant at her throat glowed softly.

Kael splashed ahead, curls plastered to her face, jacket torn down one sleeve. She reached the truck first, fumbling with the keys.

"Passenger side's clear," she called over the rain.

He crossed the last stretch, boots sliding in the water. Kael yanked the door open.

"Set her there," she said. "I'll drive."

Erik hesitated. The pendant pulsed against Allie's skin. The light mirrored the faint shimmer still flickering beneath his sleeve.

"I've got her," he said quietly.

He slid into the seat with her still in his arms, careful not to jostle her or the box. The scent of smoke and iron clung to her hair.

Kael studied him for a moment, then shook her head. "Mara would've laughed at this," she muttered, and slammed the door before circling to the driver's side.

Erik did not respond. Rain hit the windshield in hard bursts. He looked down at Allie. Her breathing was shallow but steady. The pendant's pulse matched the rhythm beneath his ribs.

He drew his hand away, staring at the glowing marks along his forearm. The shimmer had faded to ember, but the pattern remained.

Kael's voice pulled him back. "You good?"

He blinked. "I'm fine."

Kael looked unconvinced but turned the key. The engine rumbled to life.

"You sure? You look like hell."

He said nothing, his eyes returning to Allie.

Her dark hair clung to her cheek, soaked and tangled. Her skin was cold against his hand, too pale. Her lashes twitched. For a heartbeat, Erik saw a flicker of silver-blue behind her closed eyes. It vanished as quickly as it came.

Whatever the sigil had done, it had changed her.

The pendant still glowed at her throat. Its rhythm slowed, then matched his.

"She's not only bonded," he said quietly. "She's tethered to something older."

Kael glanced at him. "Then we find out what it is before it finds us."

Erik gave a small nod. The bond tugged at him, silent and insistent.

He had no idea how she would react when she learned the truth, when she learned she had been bound to a dragon.

He remembered the quiet strength in Allie at the scene of Lena's murder. She had not flinched when the investigators tried to push her aside. She had stood her ground. And tonight, even as the world broke open around her, she had refused to back down.

The box in her arms hummed once more. Not just power. Not just magic. Recognition.

The wipers scraped across the windshield, fighting the storm. Erik turned his gaze to the dark street ahead, but his arms remained locked around Allie.

Kael did not comment.

Behind them, the alley was already fading beneath the rain.

Erik looked down at Allie one more time. Her face was pale in the shifting light. The pendant at her throat pulsed softly.

He tightened his grip.

Whatever came next, they would face it together.

CHAPTER 31

KAEL

*R*ain lashed the windshield in cold sheets. Kael leaned forward over the steering wheel, squinting into the storm. The wipers squealed in protest.

Beside her, Erik sat crumpled in the passenger seat, shoulders bowed around the unconscious weight in his arms.

Allie's face was pale against his chest, her breath barely rising. The pendant at her throat pulsed a soft golden light, slow and steady.

Kael glanced at them again. Erik's scars glowed faintly beneath his skin. Gold shimmer traced his neck and arms. Wherever his skin touched Allie's, the light flared brighter.

They were bonded now. Not halfway. Full ignition.

The steering wheel vibrated under her hands. She risked another glance.

Erik had not moved or spoken since they pulled Allie from the wrecked office. His hands stayed locked around her.

Kael exhaled slowly and adjusted her mirror. The rain was coming harder now. The storm was following them.

That was not a metaphor.

"Of course it is," she muttered.

She took the next turn hard, tires screeching as the truck fishtailed before finding grip.

Erik finally blinked. "Where are we?" he rasped.

"Almost there," Kael said. "Safe house."

He looked down at Allie, brushing a wet curl from her temple. "She is burning through it too fast. The bond, the pendant, whatever that power was. It's still in her."

Kael nodded once. "Yes. I feel it too. It hasn't settled yet."

"She needs help," he said.

"I know. But not from the Alliance. Not this time."

Erik did not argue. That scared her more than shouting would have.

Kael turned off the main road, tires bumping over cracked asphalt. The jazz club looked like it had drowned a century ago. Boarded windows. A rusted sign. Graffiti curling up the walls.

She pulled around back and cut the engine. For a moment, silence pressed in.

She opened the door. Rain hit her face, sharp and cold. She looked back.

"Let's go. We might not have long."

Kael hauled the steel door open, hinges protesting. The air beyond was stale, heavy with mildew, but it was dry and warded.

She flicked her fingers and sent a sharp gust rolling through the corridor.

"Still better than outside," she muttered.

Behind her, Erik followed. He moved like a man stitched together by adrenaline alone.

Kael reached the old elevator shaft and keyed in the sequence. The metal gate slid open, and they stepped into the lift.

"Basement is sealed," she said. "No one can track us here."

Erik stayed silent, every muscle locked on holding Allie upright.

The lift shuddered down. When it stopped, Kael led the way out into the dark. With a wave of her hand, old lanterns flared to life along the stone corridor.

The safe house was not pretty. Concrete walls. Iron reinforcements. But it was hidden and protected.

Erik crossed the room and laid Allie gently on the cot in the corner. The mattress dipped beneath her. Her hair clung in damp spirals to her cheek. The blackened box was trapped between her arms, its surface warm but silent.

Her pendant flickered once, then again. The pulses were slower now. Kael knelt beside the cot and pressed her palm to Allie's forehead.

"Still burning," she whispered. "But not as hot. She is stabilizing."

Erik did not move.

Kael stood and turned to him. "You need to sit down. You are going to fall over."

He shook his head. "I'm fine."

"You're not," she said. "Your scars are still glowing. You bonded under a magical collapse, Erik. That's not nothing."

He looked ready to argue, then did not.

Kael stepped toward the cot. "I need to take the pendant off her. The power is still feeding through it."

Erik blocked her without thinking.

Kael stopped short. "You think I would hurt her?"

"No," he said. "I think you will wake her. And if she wakes up panicked, it will feed the bond again."

Kael stepped back. "Okay. We wait."

Erik sat. Finally. But not far. He never took his eyes off her.

Kael leaned against the far wall, arms crossed.

The bond had anchored. Not a passing spark but a root driven deep. There would be no undoing it.

The Alliance would kill for this kind of fusion. The Watchers would kill to prevent it. And Erik would bleed for her.

The part that was not obvious was what Allie would do. Because Allie had not chosen this.

The storm outside softened to a steady hiss. Kael's eyes grew heavy. Across the room, Erik had drifted down beside the cot, his eyes half open but unfocused.

For a few hours, the world went quiet and let them rest.

CHAPTER 32

ALLIE

*D*arkness came first. Not absence, but weight.

Then the sound. Not thunder. Not wind. A heartbeat, too loud, too close.

It shook through her like a second pulse, not her own. She tried to breathe, but the air folded inward.

Light shimmered above her, gold bleeding into silver. It spiraled slowly, then shattered.

Then came the voices.

You were meant to remember.

And to forgive.

Shapes moved beyond the light. Wings. Scales. Hands that reached without touching. Something vast stirred beneath it.

The fire burns without permission. The storm answers without question. You are both. You are neither.

The voices fell away like a tide. Then light spilled, sudden and full.

The glen appeared. The one from her first vision. Serena stood in its center, golden hair floating in the wind that flowed through it, her skin cracked with golden light. Auren stood beside her, one hand on her shoulder, his eyes hollow fire, his palm black with ash.

But another figure moved behind them. A woman in the shadows. Lena.

Not as she was, but something deeper. Brighter. Her gaze met Allie's.

"You were never meant to bear it," Lena said gently. "But I would not let it claim you as it did me."

The wind changed. The glen rippled.

Behind Lena, something stirred. Dark and endless.

Tell her nothing is finished. Tell her the dead are watching.

Allie reached out. The light fractured.

The glen shattered, and something else rose.

She stood inside a circle of stone. The edges burned. Storms gathered above her. Wings circled in the clouds.

A child walked ahead. Barefoot. Unburned. Carrying a basket.

The child stopped and turned. Small hands lifted the basket's lid.

Inside: a brooch and a crown with a blue stone. The light from them pulsed.

The crown shimmered, its form unstable. For a heartbeat, it was gold. Then a pen. Then the pendant at her throat. The same object, wearing different shapes.

Seven shadows stood in the distance. Three were fading. One was broken. One burned with inner fire. One wore feathers. One held a blade. The seventh watched her in silence.

A new voice spoke. Ancient.

You are not the end. You are a part of the answer.

The wind howled. Her heartbeat matched it.

Then the circle fell away. She plummeted through light and storm until only one sound remained.

A heartbeat. Warm. Steady. It was not hers.

The vision fractured. Then came the cold.

Rain pressed against her skin, pulling her back.

She blinked into the dark. Her chest ached.

Something pressed against her ribs. The box. Her fingers were still locked around it.

Her first words came barely above a whisper. "I saw her. I think I saw her."

The sound of her own voice startled her. It did not feel like hers anymore.

CHAPTER 33

ALLIE

The world came back slowly. Rain hissed against stone somewhere above. Then came the faint hum of a lantern. The air smelled of old concrete and dust.

Allie opened her eyes.

The light was dim. The ceiling above her was cracked. Something warm pressed against her wrist. She turned her head, and froze.

Erik Varg sat beside the cot.

The man from the investigation. The private investigator outside the Black Cat. She remembered his eyes that night, how they had found hers even through the chaos. And the courthouse too. He had been there, watching from the back of the room.

Now he sat only inches away, his coat discarded, exhaustion carved into every line of his face. Faint patterns traced his skin, like gold beneath the surface.

Her pulse quickened.

"What are you..." she began, but the words caught.

He looked at her. "You're safe," he said quietly.

His voice was low and rough. It was meant to be steady, but something beneath it trembled.

She pushed herself upright, hands shaking. The world tilted.

A shadow moved at the edge of her vision. Another figure stepped closer.

A woman, maybe a few years older than Erik, moved with easy confidence. Her hair was light and tangled, her eyes a pale, unsettling gold.

"Easy," the woman said. "Go slow."

Allie stared. "Who are you?"

"Kael," she said simply. "A friend. I knew Mara."

The name struck hard. Kael. Allie had seen that name in Mara's journal.

Her breath caught. She looked around. Concrete walls. Lantern light. No windows. A single heavy door bolted shut behind them.

Her gaze dropped to her lap. The blackened box rested there. Relief and dread collided. She ran her fingers over the lid. It was warm. Reaching into her pocket, she felt the brooch, then touched the pendant at her throat. Its faint pulse still beat.

Every piece was here.

"Where am I?" she asked.

"Safe house," Kael said. "Old warded building."

"Warded? Like magic?"

Kael's gaze held steady. "Exactly like magic."

Allie waited for one of them to laugh. Neither did.

She looked back at Erik. "You're the investigator. From the Black Cat."

He nodded once. "Yes."

Her thoughts jumped back to the office. Detective Hargrove. The desk glowing red. The fire.

"You were at the bar?" she asked. "You followed me?"

"I was outside," he said. "When it happened."

"Then why'm I here?"

Neither answered immediately. Kael's gaze shifted toward Erik.

"What happened?" Allie asked.

Kael folded her arms. "Tell us what you remember first."

"The office," Allie said slowly. "I was retrieving my sister's box.

Hargrove came in. He had a vial. He poured it onto the desk, and a mark started to glow. Then it went wrong. He melted."

Her voice cracked. "It's strange, but he didn't see me. There was light. It filled the room, and then... nothing."

Erik's expression darkened.

She felt his hand then, still on her arm. The warmth sank through her skin and reached something in her that should not have answered. A rhythm that did not belong to either of them alone.

A thought flickered at the edge of her mind. Not words. Just an impression. Tension. Guilt.

I tried to save you.

Allie's breath caught. "Save me from what?"

Erik froze. Kael's head tilted. "What?"

"You. I heard you say something."

"I didn't speak," Erik said.

Kael's gaze moved between them. "That's new. And not a good sign."

Allie shook her head. "What's happening to me?"

Kael sighed. "You know anything about dragons?"

Erik shot her a look. Kael ignored it.

Allie blinked. "Dragons? You mean like fairy tales?"

Kael did not smile. Erik said nothing. The silence was heavier than denial.

Allie's mouth went dry. "You can't be serious."

"You tell me," Kael said.

Erik looked away, the muscle in his jaw tightening.

Allie opened her mouth to argue, but the warmth at her collarbone surged. It pulsed once, sharp enough to steal her breath. Erik flinched at the same moment, as if he felt it too.

Her hand flew to the mark beneath her skin.

"What's that?" she whispered.

Neither answered.

Something cold slid down her spine. "Tell me," she said. "Right now."

Erik hesitated. Too long.

Her pulse thundered. She saw Erik reacting to it, his own breath hitching as hers accelerated.

"You're telling me we're connected in some way."

Her voice was calm. Too calm. The kind that came just before something broke.

Erik nodded once. Carefully.

"The bond formed during..."

"I know when it formed." Her eyes did not move. "What I want to know is how to undo it."

Silence stretched thin.

"Can it be undone?" she pressed.

Kael spoke from the doorway. "There are rituals that can test whether breaking it is possible, but they require both parties to consent. Removing the bond isn't likely to work. It's never been accomplished. And failure usually means death."

Allie turned to Erik.

"Would you? Consent to testing?"

He met her eyes.

"If that's what you want."

"That is not an answer."

A breath.

"Yes. If you want it broken, I'll do whatever it takes."

Something in her expression shifted. Not softening. Not warming. Just recognition.

"I didn't choose this," she said quietly. "I didn't choose any of this. Watchers. Magic. Dragons. You." She pressed her palm to her chest, where the bond glowed beneath her skin. "This thing between us? It's not real. It's proximity. Magic. Aftershock."

"Maybe," Erik said softly. "Or maybe the bond only activated and saved your life because of magic and because something was already there."

"You don't know that."

"No. But neither do you."

She looked away.

"I need time."

"Then take it," Erik said.

Kael exhaled once. "Unfortunately, time is the one thing we don't have. Bond or no bond, you two need to work together."

Allie's jaw tightened. She looked at Erik again.

"Fine. We work together. But Erik?"

She stepped closer, just enough for him to feel the heat of her anger.

"Don't confuse necessity with choice. And don't confuse a bond with trust."

She walked past him toward the only door she could see. It shut behind her with a soft click.

The bathroom was small. Concrete and shadow. A rusted sink beneath a cracked mirror. The single light hummed, flickering.

She turned the faucet. Water sputtered, then cleared.

She braced her hands on the sink. Her fingers were shaking.

She looked pale. Her hair clung in damp strands to her face. But it was the rest that made her throat close.

Her pendant glowed faintly at her collarbone, pulsing in rhythm with her heart. Each beat sent a shimmer up her neck. She pressed her palm against it. The warmth did not fade.

For an instant, her reflection did not match her. The woman staring back had eyes touched with light, pale blue like lightning. The flicker vanished when she blinked.

"No," she whispered.

She splashed water on her face. It hit cold and sharp. When she looked again, the edges of her reflection still shimmered.

The box sat on the counter beside the sink, humming faintly. Her hand hovered over it. She did not open it.

Instead, she unfastened the pendant and set it beside the box. The hum deepened. The light between them grew stronger.

Allie took a step back.

A memory surfaced. Lena had said it one night at the bar. *Magic doesn't just change you. It shows you what you already are.*

She touched the faint mark beneath her collarbone. It pulsed once, then sank back.

She picked up the pendant and fastened it again around her neck.

She did not know how long she sat there before she realized the storm outside had changed.

It was no longer pounding against the walls.

It was circling.

And for the first time, she was not sure it was entirely outside at all.

CHAPTER 34

ERIK

The sound of the door closing echoed. Erik stayed where he was, hands in his pockets, eyes on the space Allie had just passed through. The pendant's faint glow had dimmed when she left, but the warmth beneath his skin had not.

"That went well," Kael said dryly.

"She's right," Erik said. "She didn't choose this. I'd be angry too."

Kael watched him for a long moment. "She's not alone in that either."

"The question," she said, "is whether you can earn her trust before the curse kills you both."

Erik had no answer.

Kael leaned against the far wall, arms crossed. "She believes you. At least the part she can't explain."

Erik rubbed the heel of his hand over his face. "She's terrified."

"She should be." Kael's voice stayed even. "She saw a man melt in front of her, then woke up with a dragon's heartbeat under her skin."

He said nothing. The air still carried a charge, not just from the storm but from whatever the bond had stirred between them.

Kael pushed off the wall and began to pace. "You said she reached back?"

143

"She did," Erik said. "When the sigil imploded, I tried to pull her clear. But she pulled too. The magic didn't just bind us. It recognized us."

Kael's steps slowed. "Recognized?"

"The light didn't fight her. It folded around her like it knew her name."

Kael reached for her sax case, fingers brushing the brass. "Then the sigil didn't rewrite her. It revealed her."

The words settled between them.

Erik looked up. "You think she's descended from Serena's line."

"I think something in that circle knew her. That kind of reaction doesn't happen without blood." She glanced toward the hallway. "And you think so too."

His jaw tightened. "The curse did this. Morna's legacy."

Kael nodded slowly. She looked at the desk where the box had rested. Even with it gone, the air shimmered faintly, and the wood still held a circular scorch mark.

"The artifacts are curious," she said. "They respond to her. And they echo you through her."

Erik frowned. "So what happens when she opens the box again?"

"You need to be with her when she does. If the bond is as strong as I think, it might show you more if you touch it together."

He swallowed. "And if it doesn't?"

Kael looked at the bathroom door. "Then we learn the hard way."

Outside, the storm had softened to a restless wind. A long silence passed between them.

Kael stepped away from the wall. "I need to go."

Erik turned to her. "Go where?"

"The bar. Her car's still there. If the Watchers find it first, she's exposed."

He shook his head. "It isn't safe."

"Nothing about this is. But you staying here with her is the better gamble."

He did not argue.

144

"I'll take the back streets," Kael said. "Use the wind to mask my scent. I'll be quick."

He hesitated, then nodded. "Be careful."

Kael gave one last glance toward the bathroom door. "She's stronger than you think. But strength doesn't keep you from breaking."

She turned, slung the sax over her shoulder, and opened the steel door with a sweep of her hand. The wards shimmered and let her pass.

Then she was gone.

Erik sat in the quiet, listening to the hum that was not his own heartbeat.

He laid his hand over the place on his forearm where the scars pulsed faintest. The bond still threaded there, reaching toward Allie through stone and silence. Still present. Still warm.

He could feel her in the next room. The sound of water running layered with a second awareness, quiet and insistent.

He closed his eyes and tried to give her privacy.

Outside, the wind shifted.

CHAPTER 35

KAEL

The city felt wrong.

Even before Kael left the safe house, the air pressed close. But here, the wind moved. It curled around her shoulders like a familiar hand.

She closed her eyes and let it lift the edge of her hood. The air had always known her name. It had known her since childhood, since before she could speak, when Torvald carried her up to the northern cliffs and told her to listen.

She whispered a greeting. The breeze answered.

She stepped out of the alley and let the current rise beneath her. For a moment, the storm lifted her above the rooftops. The city stretched beneath her, slick and silver.

She landed near The Black Cat.

Smoke reached her first. The truck was gone. But Allie's scent lingered, sharp with metal and rain. It pulled toward the café across the street.

Allie's car sat beside the curb. Kael touched the hood. Cold. But beneath the metal, a hum answered her fingertips. Fresh. Recent. Power clung there like static.

She looked toward the café.

Something was wrong. The angle of the doorway. The shadow across the windows. The air itself held its breath.

The café was a wreck. Shattered glass littered the threshold. The doorway had blackened around the frame. The air stank of stone and lightning.

Kael stepped inside. The wind hesitated behind her.

A sigil marked the floor, burned deep. Its edges still smoked. Not a summoning circle. An inverted one. Whoever drew it had tried to hold something in, not call it forth.

She knelt and traced one curve.

"Containment," she murmured. "Or interruption."

A glint caught her eye. A tether stone lay cracked near the wall, split clean through. Only one rune remained legible.

Gate.

Her stomach tightened.

The wind shifted behind her.

Cold rolled across the floor, but she had not called it.

"You can come out," she said. "I don't like being followed."

A familiar voice answered from the doorway.

"You never did."

Kael's spine straightened.

Torvald stepped into the light. His coat was untouched by rain. His face calm. But something in his eyes was tired, older than she remembered.

"Uncle," she said quietly.

His gaze flicked from the ruined sigil to the cracked stone. "I thought you left the Alliance. Yet here you are."

"You're not welcome near me," she said.

"I didn't come for you. I came because the residue carried on the wind. I felt it from two districts away." He exhaled. "Erik is one of mine. When he disappears after a sigil breach, I notice."

"So this is about him."

"It's always about him," Torvald said softly. "And now, it seems, about the girl."

Kael folded her arms. "Her name is Allie."

"I don't care what her name is," Torvald replied. "Is she contained?"

Kael stared at him. "She's stable."

"That wasn't my question."

"She's not a threat."

"A civilian triggered a magical collapse powerful enough to register on Alliance sensors across three states. That's the definition of a threat."

"She didn't know what she was doing."

"Which makes her more dangerous, not less." His tone softened. Not much. Enough to be noticed. "Kael. You know the protocol. Unregistered power of that magnitude requires immediate assessment. Bring her in."

Kael's breath steadied.

"No."

The silence that followed was colder than the wind.

"Excuse me?"

"I said no. She's not going to the Alliance."

"This isn't a request," he said. "Command has already…"

"I don't care what Command wants."

Torvald's expression shifted. Warning. Worry. Something older. "Kael. Think very carefully about what you're saying."

"I've thought about it."

She looked back toward the safe house in her mind. At Allie, unconscious and shaking. At Erik sitting beside her, hand wrapped around hers, as if he could anchor both of them to the same world.

Three years ago, she had been in that same place. Staring at a hospital bed. Waiting for Mara.

"Three years ago, I followed orders," Kael said. "I reported what I saw at the crash. I told you the Watchers were involved. And you told me to let it go."

"The situation was complex," Torvald said softly.

"The situation was that my best friend died, and the Alliance did nothing. You did nothing." Her voice cracked. Just once. "So no, Uncle. I'm not bringing Allie in. Not to be assessed. Not to disappear like Mara did."

"Mara's death was ruled accidental," Torvald said.

"We both know that's a lie."

His jaw tightened. He looked away first.

"If you defy a direct order," he said quietly, "there will be consequences. Your position. Your standing. Your bloodline obligations..."

"My bloodline?" Kael laughed. A sharp, bitter sound. "You mean the dynasty you want me to rebuild? The Wind-born line? Let me be very clear, Uncle. I don't give a damn about carrying on anything. Not anymore."

He absorbed the blow without flinching. But it hurt him. She saw it.

"You're making a mistake," he murmured.

"Maybe," she said. "But it's mine to make."

"They'll come for her anyway. With or without you. And when the Alliance and the Watchers feel this? They won't come to question. They'll come to burn."

Kael's hand drifted to the wind-stone fixed beneath her saxophone case.

"If they come for her," she said quietly, "they'll have to go through me."

Something in Torvald's face softened. As if he saw the child she once was. The one he had carried on his shoulders through the mountain passes. The one who had believed the Alliance existed to protect the innocent.

"Kael," he said, almost pleading.

"Tell Command whatever you want," she said. "Tell them I've gone rogue. Tell them I'm compromised. I don't care."

The wind curled tighter around her ankles.

"Mara died because I followed orders," she whispered. "Because I was a good soldier. Because I believed the Alliance knew best."

She looked toward the shattered doorway, toward the storm gathering outside.

"Not this time."

Torvald did not move to stop her.

When she stepped past him, her shoulder brushed his.

He closed his eyes, only for a moment, as if letting her go cost something.

Outside, the storm lifted her once more.

The wind-stone flared.

Allie's car waited where she had left it. With a word, Kael called the wind. The vehicle rolled free of the floodwater.

She slipped behind the wheel.

Halfway back to the safe house, the wards whispered. Something old and hungry had followed.

Kael tightened her grip on the steering wheel.

"Not tonight."

The storm folded around the car, erasing scent and sound.

The city swallowed her passage.

CHAPTER 36

TORVALD

The silence returned slowly after Kael left.

The wind she had stirred still spun through the broken café. For a long moment, Torvald did not move. Beneath the storm and the rain, the city hummed with the faint rhythm of a bond newly forged.

So Erik had done it after all.

Torvald stepped closer to the circle, stopping just short of its edge. The symbols were nearly erased. Only the sigil for gate remained, glowing faintly through the soot. He crouched and pressed his fingertips to the floor. The residue of the spell bit at his skin.

The air here was heavy. It was not simply a failed ritual. Something had answered.

He straightened and brushed the ash from his gloves.

"So this is where it broke."

The wind answered with a low hiss, fading into the rain.

He turned his gaze to the wall, where shattered glass still clung. Through it, the street stretched empty, slick with water.

Torvald reached into his coat and withdrew a small communication stone. He whispered a single word. The runes brightened with pale green light.

"Report," came a voice from the stone, filtered and cold.

Torvald studied the fading circle as he spoke.

"Containment breach confirmed at the Black Cat perimeter. Two signatures involved. Fire-born and unidentified secondary."

"Alliance property compromised?"

He hesitated, then lied. "No artifacts recovered. Local interference contained. Civilian casualties none."

The voice paused. "And Agent Varg?"

"Alive," Torvald said. "Unstable, but alive."

"Retrieve him."

"Copy," he said, though he had no plans to obey. Not yet.

The connection flickered, then died. He slipped the stone back into his pocket. His gaze moved once more to the tether stone half buried in the debris. The rune for gate was nearly gone now.

He murmured, "A gate doesn't open itself."

And yet something had pushed from the other side.

He turned away and moved toward the door.

Outside, the storm had quieted, but the air still trembled. Somewhere beyond, the girl was alive, bound to Erik's fire, carrying the weight of something the world was never meant to remember.

A voice stirred behind him, almost human, but not.

"It never stopped," it said.

He did not turn. "You're late."

The air shimmered. A figure took shape beside the ruined café, cloaked in shadow, eyes burning silver beneath a hood.

"We were watching," the figure said. "The Watchers always watch."

Torvald's smile returned.

"She shouldn't exist."

"No," Torvald agreed. "But neither should I."

The Watcher's gaze flicked toward the dying sigil. "What do you intend to do?"

"Nothing. For now."

The Watcher's shape began to fade back into mist. "And the girl?"

"She's not for you."

The wind rose again, carrying his words into the rain.
When the street fell silent once more, Torvald was gone.
Only the circle remained, its faint light sinking into the earth.

CHAPTER 37

ALLIE

The bathroom was small and dim, a single bulb flickering above the sink. The mirror was cracked. The air smelled of rust and old water.

She pressed her back to the door and waited for her breath to even out. Dragons. Bonds. Magic. It all felt too big, like it might split her open from the inside.

The blackened box sat on the counter where she had left it. No bigger than a jewelry case. Its edges were scarred but intact. The hum beneath its surface had quieted, yet she still felt it.

Her sister's letter to Lena was inside. And the journal. And the other pendant. She had placed them in the box before hiding from Hargrove. She had kept it close ever since.

Every time she touched the box, the air seemed to shift. Sometimes she swore she could hear voices caught inside.

There was something else too. The book. The one Eleanor had given her before everything began to unravel. Eleanor had handed it to her without ceremony. *Keep this safe*, she had said. *You'll know when to open it.*

But that book was still in her briefcase. And the briefcase was still in the car. And the car was still at the bar.

She pushed the thought aside. One thing at a time.

She turned on the faucet. The pipes groaned before cold water spilled out. She cupped her hands and splashed her face.

For a moment she stared at the water pooling in the sink. At the courthouse it had rippled without her touching it. In the office, frost had spread from her pen.

She needed one thing she could control. Just one.

Allie extended her hand over the water. Focused on the cold. On the memory of ice.

Move.

The water shivered. Ripples spread outward in slow, deliberate rings.

Her breath caught. She had done that. On purpose.

A sharp pain bloomed behind her eyes, pressure gathering like a storm behind bone. She winced and pulled her hand back.

The pendant at her throat warmed against her skin. Not burning. Just present. Watching.

Magic had a cost. She could feel the price collecting behind her eyes.

She pressed her palm to her forehead. The ache faded after a moment, leaving only a dull throb.

Then the hum returned.

Soft at first. A vibration that climbed from her fingertips to her wrist. She looked down. The water in the sink rippled outward from the box. Tiny rings of motion, gold and silver.

The air tightened. The room felt like it was holding its breath.

"Stop," she whispered. "Please stop."

The box ignored her.

It pulsed once. Then again. Her pendant stirred in response, light spilling across her collarbone.

Then a voice curled into her thoughts.

Allie. What are you doing?

She jerked her head toward the door. Nothing. The voice had not come from outside. It was inside her, woven through the bond.

Her vision shimmered. Her heartbeat tangled with his voice until she could not tell which was hers. Somewhere inside that voice she felt concern, and that made it worse.

The bond thrummed. Her pendant flared again. Before she could stop herself, her hand moved.

Her fingers brushed the lid.

The latch clicked open.

The door crashed open behind her.

Erik.

He moved fast. His boots struck the tile. His presence filled the space, sharp with urgency and fear.

He reached for her. "Don't," he said, his voice raw.

But it was too late.

The lid opened.

The box answered.

The pendant flared in response, silver light spilling across her skin. The bond ignited.

Heat surged up her arm, sharp and searing. Her ears filled with a roar. The floor vanished. For a breathless instant she came apart, reduced to light and breath.

Erik's hand found hers, grounding her just as the magic detonated.

Then the vision took shape.

CHAPTER 38

ERIK

*E*rik paced the hallway outside the bathroom, jaw clenched, hands restless. The bond thrummed beneath his skin, pulling at him with every breath she took on the other side of the door.

He had tried to give her space. Tried to let her sort through it without crowding her, but the magic between them did not know how to wait.

She had been too quiet.

He reached for the bond again. Not fully, not like before, but enough to feel for her presence.

It hit him in the chest. A flicker, then a jolt.

Panic. Rising fast.

The box.

His breath stilled. He stepped forward and pressed his palm flat to the door.

"Allie?"

No answer.

The hum grew sharper.

Then her pulse leapt. The bond surged.

Silver light spilled under the door.

He moved.

The door gave under his shoulder with a sharp crack. The world narrowed to the glow around her hands. The box on the counter. Her fingers hovering just above the lid.

Erik saw her hand move before she did.

The moment her skin brushed the surface, something inside the bond snapped taut. A pulse shot through him.

The box flared. So did she.

He crossed the room in a breath, catching her wrist just as the latch clicked.

Too late.

The lid opened.

The air went still.

Erik felt it hit. Not just in the room, but somewhere deeper. The same pressure he had felt in the bar, in the alley, in the ash-filled wind.

Only this time, it knew him back.

He gripped her wrist tighter as the vision dragged her under. He should have let go.

He did not.

The bond flared, blinding and absolute. Her light. His fire. Entangled.

Then he was no longer standing.

The safe house vanished.

And he fell into fire.

The burned glen slammed into view. Familiar, though he could not say why.

She stood at the center, already facing the sigil.

But Erik's eyes were drawn elsewhere.

The edges of the circle.

The runes burned too cleanly. Too recent.

Not a memory.

A tether.

And in the smoke behind the shadowed woman, something moved. A flicker of wings. A large shape, barely human.

CHAPTER 39

ALLIE

A glen stretched out before her.

Not green. Not alive. Burned.

The trees were blackened spires. Ash coated the ground. Everything felt scorched.

Erik stood beside her. He scanned the space, jaw tight. Recognition flickered across his features.

"This is a memory," he said quietly. "But not yours. It's anchored to something unfinished."

At the center of the glen stood a woman cloaked in shadow. Smoke coiled around her. Her hands were bare, glowing with sigils edged in gold and red.

"What is she doing?" Allie asked, her voice shaking.

Erik's gaze narrowed. "Look at the sigil. It's folding in on itself. She's not casting. She's trying to unmake something that was already bound. That's what it looks like when a bond dies."

Allie stared, breath hitching. "I know this place."

He turned to her.

"I've been here before," she said softly. "In dreams. But it wasn't burned then. I saw a little girl. And a dragon."

"You saw the bond's origin?" His voice faltered. "That's not just impossible..."

He stepped closer, studying her face. The light from the sigils touched her eyes. They glowed faintly gold. His own caught the same light in return.

"Allie," he said. "Your eyes."

Before she could respond, the woman in the glen lifted her head.

Her face sharpened. Not Morna. Not Serena. Someone else. Younger. Her eyes blazed with fury and grief.

She spoke, but no sound reached them. The earth answered instead.

Symbols flared around her feet. The same sigil from the alley. From Lena's office. But this one was inverted.

The air screamed.

"She's trying to break it," Erik said. "That's a bonded circle."

He pointed to the center, where a second light pulsed. Faint. Steady. Alive.

"There. Her counterpart. Fireborn. She's storm. He's flame."

The sigil buckled inward. The air split. Pressure hit like a wall and drove Allie to her knees. Heat burst from the circle.

A man appeared within the light. His body burned from the inside, flame rising from his skin. The markings on his arms mirrored her own, glowing in the same rhythm.

"They are bonded," Erik said quietly. "And it is killing them."

The woman reached for him. The magic tore through her instead. A strand of white light snapped midstream. The rupture did not explode.

It collapsed.

Light drained from the air. The glen seemed to fold inward for a breathless moment.

Something left her. She fell without impact.

A street sign flickered through the air. Allie reached toward it without meaning to. The letters rearranged themselves behind her eyes.

Then everything went white.

She screamed.

The vision tore apart.

Her body hit cold tile. The box slammed shut between her hands.

Her lungs locked. She could not breathe. Her chest seized once, then again. She curled forward, choking.

Erik caught her before she collapsed. "Let it go," he whispered. "Let it pass."

She could not answer. Her throat burned.

She convulsed once, then doubled over.

Water and bile spilled from her mouth, faintly silver and steaming. The scent of rain and iron filled the air.

Erik knelt beside her, arms steady around her frame. His marks glowed in sync with hers.

The hum faded. Her vision dimmed. Her strength drained.

Silence pressed in. For a long moment there was only the sound of dripping water and her pulse trying to remember rhythm.

Her palm closed around something warm.

When her fingers uncurled, the brooch lay there.

The dragon scale gleamed, wet and iridescent. Faint violet fire shimmered along its surface. It pulsed once, answering the light in her pendant.

The box hummed once, low and pleased.

In the quiet that followed, the air no longer smelled like rust.

It smelled like rain.

Then silence.

CHAPTER 40

ERIK

The air in the bathroom still shimmered with heat, though the magic had drained from it.

Erik sat with Allie slumped against him, her breathing ragged against his chest. Her skin was clammy, her fingers twitching. The connection between them slid under his skin, wild and uneven.

He tightened his arms around her and let out a breath. The vision had cracked something open in both of them.

Carefully, he gathered her up and carried her through the narrow hall into the small bedroom. The bed creaked under her weight as he laid her down. She did not stir.

The pendant still glowed faintly at her collarbone. So did the brooch, now curled into her palm.

He brushed damp hair from her face, his hand trembling.

"I should end this," he whispered.

But he did not move.

He sat instead on the edge of the bed and watched her breathe.

His mother had burned for days after her bond collapsed. Not in flame, but inside. A slow scorching that left her hollow. He had seen the sigils she carved into the floorboards, the same broken rune drawn again and again. She had told him once, *love should never be a weapon, Erik. But I made it one.*

The sigil in the vision had not simply collapsed. It had fought. It had screamed. Whatever the woman had tried to do, it had become their undoing.

He turned the pieces over in his mind.

The curse. The prophecy. Fire and storm will break the curse.

Then why the dead?

Death-sigils were old, cruel things. Even in wartime, they had been avoided.

But the librarian would know. He had studied blood-sigils, death magic, even bond collapses.

Erik looked at Allie again, pale, still, fragile in a way she had never looked before.

That woman in the glen had not merely lost someone. She had loved him, and it had destroyed them both.

He had sworn he would never let that happen.

That terrified him more than the fire.

A faint clink drew his attention.

The brooch in her hand had shifted, catching the low light.

He gently pried it free, and the moment his fingers touched the metal, it pulsed. Cold and deliberate. Like it remembered him.

He turned it over. It looked like a scale. Old. The magic in it was older still.

And now it was in Allie's possession, pulsing as if it knew them. As if it had chosen them.

He held it a moment longer.

"Not my fault," he muttered.

The brooch pulsed once in reply.

He looked at Allie again. She had no idea what she was carrying. Neither did he.

He reached for her other hand and wrapped it in his.

Not to protect. Not even to promise.

Just to stay.

CHAPTER 41

ALLIE

*A*llie woke in the bedroom. Her heart pounded. The scent of smoke clung to her hair.

For a long moment she did not move. Did not breathe.

The box sat on the nightstand, closed now. Silent. But her hands still remembered the heat of it.

A low hum came from the far wall where the ward runes pulsed faintly. Erik stood near them, arms crossed. He had not noticed she was awake.

Allie shifted to the edge of the bed, hands knotted in the blanket.

Her skin still tingled. Not with pain, but with something stranger. Like the echo of something that had fallen out of hearing.

She could still see it. The candle. The sigil. The ring of stones.

Light it, and the chain remembers.

"How long was I out?"

He turned. His expression softened, but the tension in his shoulders did not ease.

"Ten minutes. Maybe."

She rubbed her face and groaned. "Feels like I got drop-kicked by a god."

169

"Could've been worse. You're alive."

She gave him a sideways look. "Debatable."

Then, softer, "I had a dream."

He stilled.

"There was a circle. Stone floor. Sigils carved into it. Six candles. Five were lit, red, blue, green, white, and violet. One stood in the center, dark, waiting."

She swallowed. "A voice said, 'Light it, and the chain remembers.'"

The memory struck in flashes. Silver flame. Blinding light. Cracked stone.

"I lit it anyway." Her eyes met his. "I didn't hesitate."

She stared off. "Six candles… six comes up a lot." Her voice softened, more thought than question. "I wonder if it means something."

Erik was silent for a long moment, then exhaled. "Six marks. Six elements."

His eyes found hers. "In the old texts, that pattern was only ever used for one thing."

"What?"

"Resurrection. Or restoration of what was lost."

The words settled between them. The air felt thinner, as if something unseen had just turned to look at her.

Three days ago, she had found Lena's body.

Two days ago, she had walked away from everything she thought was real.

And now this.

She pressed her palms to her eyes. The image burned behind them.

"I saw her. The woman in the glen. I felt everything. Like something was breaking."

Erik's gaze sharpened. "Breaking how?"

"She was holding on to something. Someone. There was light, and the sound of the world tearing."

He did not speak right away. When he did, his voice was low.

"Something stirred. I felt it too. The bond."

She lowered her hands. "So, what am I now?"

He looked at her for a long time.

"Changed. Bound. But not broken."

"No. I mean, what am I?" Her voice cracked. "You said I'm not fully human."

"You carry dragon blood. That much is certain." A pause. "But I don't think that's the whole story."

He sat beside her.

"You survived a death sigil. Redirected it. That kind of power isn't typical."

Her throat tightened. "So, I shouldn't be alive."

He hesitated. "Most wouldn't be."

She stared at the floor. "This is insane."

He ran a hand through his hair. "There's a legend. Auren and Serena. Their bond was different. Some say they passed it on."

She blinked. "I heard those names. In the vision."

He turned to her. "Then it's not coincidence. Something in your blood remembers."

Her gaze drifted to the nightstand. The pendant still shimmered faintly. The brooch lay beside it, quiet now but still pulsing in time with her breath.

"I don't think it's just my blood," she said. "The pendant. The brooch. Even the box. They react to me. Like they know me."

Erik followed her line of sight, eyes narrowing. "Artifacts don't respond like that without cause. Not unless there's a tie to the original source."

"You think they belonged to Serena?"

"It's possible. How did you get them?" He leaned forward slightly, reaching toward the brooch, careful not to touch it. His hand hovered just above the metal, close enough to feel the hum of its magic. He drew back with a faint hiss. "It remembers fire."

Allie hesitated. "Mara. The box, I mean. She left it for me with Lena. The brooch was inside, along with her journal. The pendant... that came from Mara as well, but Lena had it. She gave it to me the day she died. She called it a key, and it's what opened the box."

Erik's jaw tightened at the mention of her sister. He looked again at the artifacts. "Then they weren't random. These things were passed down for a reason. Someone was trying to preserve something. Knowledge. Power. A connection. Maybe all three."

She exhaled slowly, the weight of it pressing down. "So they're not just old heirlooms."

"No," he said. "They're keys. Memory-bound. Anchored to something older than this generation. Maybe older than the Alliance."

The bond pulsed beneath her ribs. Steady. Alive. For the first time, she was not sure which heartbeat was hers.

"Are we supposed to break it now? The curse?"

"Seems likely."

He paused. *I need more information.*

She nodded once.

He froze. She had heard him. Through the bond.

"What about the rest?" she said. "The marks. The candles."

"Four are complete," Erik said. "Each tied to an element. The pattern's accelerating."

Her stomach dropped. "What happens when all six are complete?"

Erik was quiet for a moment.

"When I touched your sister's medallion, I saw her final moments. She was investigating the pattern. She called it the Renewal. Said it required a vessel."

Allie's breath caught. "A vessel for what?"

"The original caster, perhaps. Morna. Or what's left of her."

The silence stretched.

"You think I'm the vessel."

"I think it is likely. The bond. The reactions. The way the magic recognizes you." He paused. "If Eleanor gave you that book, she knew what was coming."

She tried to protest, but he shook his head.

"Whatever comes next, you face it on your feet, or not at all."

He touched her shoulder, gentle, grounding.

"Sleep. Just for a while."

"I don't want to close my eyes," she whispered.

"You won't lose anything. Just time you'll need later."

The warmth of his hand moved through her. Her eyes drifted shut.

"You'll still be here?" she asked.

He did not answer with words. Just took the chair beside the bed.

Her last clear thought was of Eleanor's voice waiting in the pages of the book.

When sleep came, it was quiet.

CHAPTER 42

ERIK

The safe-house settled into silence once Allie's breathing grew steady.

Erik sat beside her bed, still in his coat. He told himself he was keeping watch. Monitoring the bond.

After a while, he stood and moved to the cot in the outer room.

He was not fooling anyone. Least of all himself.

He could feel her dreaming. Only the emotions bleeding through. Confusion. Grief. And beneath it all, determination wrapped in storm-light.

His scars pulsed faintly beneath his sleeve, gold threading through the old burns. They had been quiet for years. Now they moved like something alive.

He should leave. Check the perimeter. Do something useful.

But the bond tightened each time he considered it.

Not hers. His.

"Damn it," he whispered.

He closed his eyes, just for a moment.

The moment stretched. Exhaustion pulled at him. Before he could resist, sleep took him.

The bond hummed louder as the world dissolved.

Fire surrounded him. Controlled. His. It responded to his will, moved with his breath.

Until it did not.

The flames bent toward something beyond his reach. He turned, following their pull, and saw her.

Allie stood in the center, untouched. Storm gathered around her in spiraling bands of silver and blue.

Where flame met storm, neither consumed the other.

"You cannot fight it forever," she said.

Not Allie's voice. Older. Serena, perhaps.

"I'm not fighting it."

"Yes, you are. You think control means suppression. But bonds do not work that way. The more you pull back, the harder they pull you in."

The dream shifted.

Flashes struck:

Marcus, bound in the control tower. Blood drained from his skin.

Allie's eyes, blazing silver-blue. Storm pouring from her skin.

A woman with storm-gray hair, smiling as the world burned.

The sixth candle lit.

Everything consumed.

The visions faded.

The safe-house reformed around him. Different. Wrong in the way dreams were wrong.

Allie stood in the doorway.

Not the exhausted woman he had left sleeping. This was dream-Allie, storm-light flickering in her eyes, the pendant glowing at her throat.

"Erik," she said.

Just his name. Question and answer. Fear and certainty.

He should step back. Should wake himself.

But his feet carried him forward anyway.

The space between them collapsed. Her hand found his chest. His fingers tangled in her hair. The bond sang, no longer a gentle pulse but a roaring demand.

When their lips met, the world ignited.

Heat built between them. Not just desire, but power. His fire roared. Her storm answered.

"I'll burn you," he rasped against her mouth.

Her eyes met his, fierce. "Then let me burn."

The bond opened fully. Barriers crumbled.

He felt her fear and her desire. Her grief tangled with need.

And she felt his terror. The certainty that he would destroy her.

But beneath the fear burned something hotter.

The pendant at her throat blazed. His scars flared gold. The room erupted in light.

This is how bonds complete, he thought. This is the point of no return.

"I'll ruin you," he whispered.

Her hands framed his face. "Then ruin me."

The world went white.

A jolt ripped through him.

Erik bolted awake.

His breath came in gasps. Sheets twisted around his legs.

The safe-house was dark. Silent except for his pulse.

His hand reached for her instinctively. His fingers grasped nothing but cold air.

He pressed his palms to his face and willed his breathing to slow.

A dream. Just a dream.

His scars still burned gold beneath his sleeve.

The bond thrummed beneath his ribs.

Worse than that, he could feel her. Not only her presence in the next room.

Arousal. Confusion.

The ghost of the same dream bled through the bond.

She had felt it too.

"Damn it," he whispered.

The bond no longer connected only their thoughts. It shared everything now.

He stood and crossed to the small basin. Cold water hit his face.

Her voice still rang in his ears.

Then ruin me.

In the bedroom, Allie's breathing had shifted. Shallow. Quick. Awake.

Or pretending not to be.

Erik closed his eyes.

He could not go back in there. Not knowing what they had just shared.

He grabbed his coat with shaking hands.

Marcus. Love Field Airport Control Tower. The fifth mark. He had a job to do.

He scrawled the note in a rush:

Checking on Marcus. Back by noon. Kael's bringing your car. Stay inside. Wards are active. E

He paused at the door. Every instinct screamed to go back to her.

The bond pulled tight.

But if he stayed, if he walked back and saw her awake, her eyes holding the same hunger from the dream...

He would cross a line he could never uncross.

"I'm sorry," he whispered to the empty room.

Then he left before the bond could change his mind.

Outside, the storm gathered.

Thunder rolled low across the city.

The first drops of rain hit his face.

Somewhere ahead, the fifth mark waited.

Behind him, Allie lay awake in the dark.

Her heart raced.

The phantom heat of his touch still burned across her skin.

CHAPTER 43

ALLIE

She stared at the ceiling long after the sound of his footsteps faded.

The bond still pulsed behind her ribs, faint but constant.

She had dreamed of fire.

No.

Him.

Her hand curled into the sheets. The bond had always been strange, pulling, whispering, but this was different.

She could still feel him. Not just his presence. His hands. His mouth. The way his voice had broken when he said he would ruin her.

Then ruin me, she had said.

And she had meant it.

Her body ached as if she had truly been touched. But no one had touched her.

Not really.

Had she touched him?

She pushed the blankets aside and sat up. Her legs felt weak. Her heart pounded hard beneath her ribs.

The pendant at her throat pulsed faintly. Still warm.

And worse, he had felt it too.

She had sensed it through the connection the moment he woke. That jolt of panic. The shock of cold water.

She should have said something. Should have spoken when she felt his presence retreat.

But she had lain there, pretending sleep, because she had not known what to say.

Because if she had spoken, she would have begged him to stay.

The bond had cracked open. She did not know how to close it again.

She stood and crossed to the kitchen, where he had left the note on the table.

Checking on Marcus. Back by noon. Kael's bringing your car. Stay inside. Wards are active. E

Back by noon. It was barely past three in the morning.

She did not know whether to feel relieved or abandoned. Or irritated that he was still giving her orders.

Part of her wanted to pretend it had meant nothing. Just a dream.

But that would have been a lie.

What she had felt had been hers. And his. Shared.

The bond was no longer just magic.

Allie turned from the table and moved to the window. Outside, the storm had not broken. Rain streaked the glass in quiet threads.

She needed to think. To plan.

Eleanor. The book. The murders. Marcus.

She could not hide out here forever.

Her gaze dropped to the pendant, still glowing faintly.

The bond hummed beneath her skin.

Whatever happened when he came back, they would deal with it then.

Right now, she needed to regain her strength. She could still feel the drain lingering like a shadow under her skin.

CHAPTER 44

KAEL

The drive back took longer than it should have.

Kael had left the Black Cat with Allie's car an hour ago, Torvald's warning still fresh in her mind. Something older was watching. The words had sounded like a prophecy.

She doubled back twice, took three unnecessary turns, and watched her mirrors for headlights that never appeared.

But the feeling on the back of her neck refused to fade.

Something was following.

Not Torvald. She would have sensed him. Not the Alliance either.

This was something else.

Something patient.

The rain pounded with purpose. Her wipers dragged across the windshield. The city dissolved into smears of light and shadow.

She parked half a block from the safe-house, killed the engine, and listened. She popped the trunk before stepping out. The briefcase was there, soaked but intact. Beside it sat a small duffel. She grabbed both and slung them over her shoulder.

Just rain. Wind. The distant hum of the city waking.

Nothing else.

But her instincts screamed otherwise.

She stepped into the downpour. The wind-stone beneath her collar vibrated faintly. Not alarm. Warning.

The bond was stirring.

Kael moved quickly through the alley. The wards flickered as she approached the safe-house door.

Not good.

She pressed her palm against the sigil etched into the wall. Warmth pulsed through it, sluggish.

Someone had been here. Pushed against the wards. Tested them for weakness.

Recently.

Kael glanced back. The alley was empty. The street beyond was silent except for rain.

But the sensation remained. A weight in the air.

She knocked twice.

No answer.

"Allie," she called softly. "It's me."

Silence.

She pressed her hand to the door. The wards recognized her. Unlocked.

Inside, the air was thick with residual energy.

The lights were low. The main room was empty. Erik's coat was gone from the hook.

On the table sat a note in his sharp handwriting.

Kael stared at the final line.

Wards are active.

No. They were not.

And Erik had left Allie alone anyway.

Her jaw tightened. She understood why. Something had happened here during the night. Something raw. The bond had flared.

Erik had run.

But running left Allie vulnerable. And the wards were failing.

Kael moved to the bedroom door. Cracked it open just enough to confirm Allie was still there. Asleep.

She pulled the door closed and returned to the main room.

One last check of the perimeter.

She stepped back into the rain and froze.

A figure stood across the street, half-hidden in shadow. Too still to be coincidence.

Watching.

The energy signature hit Kael hard.

Storm-touched. Old. Powerful.

Not Torvald. Not Alliance.

Kael's hand went to the blade at her ribs, but the figure did not move. It just stood in the downpour, rain streaming down its coat.

Their eyes met across the distance.

For a single heartbeat, Kael felt the weight of that gaze. Recognition.

Then the figure turned. Slow. Deliberate.

And walked away.

Not fleeing. Just leaving.

Kael ran.

By the time she reached the spot where the figure had stood, there was nothing. No footprints. No scent. No residual magic.

Just rain pooling in the gutter.

Kael stood there, breath hard.

Elena Mendez knew where the safe-house was.

The wards were weakening.

And Erik had left Allie alone.

"Damn it," Kael whispered.

She turned back toward the safe-house. Better to circle. To draw attention away.

Kael pulled her hood up and stepped into the wind. It rose to meet her, lifting her coat.

She made three loops through the district. Elena did not follow. No Watchers waited.

Still, Kael did not trust the stillness.

She doubled back, then cut through a service alley and slipped inside through the back door of the safe-house. The sun was rising.

The wards flickered at her presence but held. Barely.

The lights were low. The main room empty.
Then a sound. Movement.
Allie was awake.
She did not say anything.
She did not have to.

CHAPTER 45

ELENA

*R*ain dripped from the edges of her hood.

The city spread out below, its lights fractured through sheets of water. Once, flame had obeyed her. Now it only mocked her.

She stood on the roof above the safe-house, listening.

The bond hummed faintly through the storm. Too bright. Too alive. She closed her eyes and let it pulse through her ruined veins.

She could taste them. The girl. The dragon. Their power braided through the dark, unbroken still.

She pressed her fingers to her temple. The pain was constant now. The old magic clawed behind her eyes. The more the bond strengthened, the more it pulled at her mind, demanding completion.

But she could not balance. Not anymore.

She had seen the fire. The moment it failed. The way it coiled back and burrowed into her flesh. The curse had not killed her. It had left her breathing, but wrong.

Not mortal. Not draconic.

Something in between.

Below, they still did not understand what they carried. They would learn.

Or they would burn.

The rain thickened. The skin on her hands shimmered faintly where the curse had branded her.

The wards around the safe-house flickered. She felt them tremble against her presence. The sigil burned faintly in her palm. She could break the barrier if she wished.

But she would not.

Not yet.

The bond needed time to ripen.

When the sixth mark appeared, when the choice came, the storm-born would understand.

And the dragon would burn.

She stepped back from the ledge. The wind caught her hood and threw rain across her face.

She turned away and walked into the storm.

Somewhere below, the fifth mark was being completed. She would feel it when it was done.

It was close now.

The city swallowed her easily.

CHAPTER 46

KILLER - MOIRA

She moved without sound.

The rain slicked her coat, but the magic under her ribs guided her feet. Erik thought she was watching from a roof. He was only incomplete.

Marcus worked late at Love Field. He always worked late.

She watched the control tower from across the access road. The building rose above the field, its windows glowing amber. The sigils in her palm pulsed. She felt the warding around the tower. Stubborn. Amateur. They groaned where she pressed.

She stepped through a service entrance where the security badge reader had been left propped open. Her fingers found the emergency stairwell.

The control room smelled of electronics and cold coffee. Screens glowed in neat rows. Marcus was alone at his station, shoulders bent over the console, headset pushed back on one ear. He hummed to himself.

He did not look up when she crossed the floor.

She waited until he reached for his coffee mug. His shoulder tightened. He straightened and turned toward her.

His eyes widened. Recognition came a second before betrayal.

"You shouldn't be here," he said.

She smiled. "Neither should you."

The blade at her hip made no sound when she drew it. He saw it then, and his hands went empty. He took a single step back.

She did not give him time.

Her movement was fast. The blade slid between ribs with a soft sound. Marcus let out a surprised breath. He tried to lift an arm. The light left his face.

She did not watch him die. She watched the way the mark took. Blood spilled onto the floor, and the sigil she carried burned where it touched the pooled liquid.

She placed her hand on his chest. The warmth she expected was absence. She pressed the sigil to his sternum. The rune answered. A small light moved over his skin, imprinting the mark. The fifth.

A sound came from the door. A shout, muffled by distance. The world had not noticed this theft yet.

She stepped back and lifted the blade. The old pain at her temple stabbed. For a moment she thought of the woman she had once been. She was gone.

She wiped the blood on his uniform shirt. The sigil on his chest still burned faintly. It answered to her thought, anchoring a line in the sequence.

She turned to leave but paused at the console. A scrap of paper fluttered. She plucked it up and smoothed it. A shift schedule.

She bent and folded it into a small square. On the scrap, she wrote with a fingertip dipped in his blood, a single curl that would mean nothing to the police, but everything to those who read sigils. She dropped the note onto the keyboard.

Outside, the rain had steadied. She walked back through the service entrance the way she had come, breathing not with relief, but with fullness.

The wound inside her thrummed, fed. The curse was less a chain than an appetite. Tonight, it had eaten.

She stepped onto the curb and looked back once. The light inside the upper windows flickered, then went steady. The overnight shift would find him in an hour.

She walked away thinking only of Morna. Each death was a tightening. When the sixth mark burned, when the choice was pressed into a chest that still remembered love, she would be there.

Tonight, she had given it Marcus.

She disappeared into the city's veins, unseen and unrepentant.

CHAPTER 47

ALLIE

*A*llie woke to pale light filtering through the narrow window. For a moment, she lay still, listening for Erik's breathing, for any sound that would tell her she was not alone.

Silence answered.

She sat up slowly. Her body ached. The pendant at her throat pulsed softly, warm against her skin.

The bond.

She pressed her palm to it and felt the echo of Erik's heartbeat somewhere beyond the walls. Distant but steady. He was alive.

The main room was empty. Erik's note still sat on the table. His handwriting told her he would be back by noon.

It was ten fifteen.

A soft creak echoed from the stairwell. She tensed.

"Easy," Kael called. "It's me."

She stepped inside, soaked from the rain. The saxophone case hung over one shoulder.

"Your car's three blocks over," Kael said. "Masked the trail best I could. Watchers were sniffing around the bar last night." She nudged the briefcase forward with her boot. "Found it in the trunk. The book held up." She tapped the duffel. "Gym bag too."

Allie pulled the briefcase into her lap. Her fingers trembled as she undid the latches.

Inside, the files were ruined. Ink bled across the pages.

Beneath the mess, wrapped in a torn scarf, was the book.

Eleanor's book.

Kael watched her. "Your aunt knew what she was giving you."

"Did she?"

Kael did not flinch. "She was Watcher-born. She knew. And she gave it to you anyway."

Allie stared at the book. The leather cover was soft with age, symbols faintly visible.

"Read it," Kael said. "I'll be checking the perimeter."

She stepped away, then paused. Her gaze shifted to the pulsing bond mark under Allie's collarbone.

"The bond," Kael said quietly. "You're going to ask what it means."

Allie's hand rose instinctively to her chest. "Yeah."

"It's a tether," Kael said, returning to the table and cleaning her blade with practiced motions. "Dragons bonded for survival. In battle, you could draw from each other's strength. Share power when one's about to fall." She set the blade down. "It kept us alive when the curse was young and we were still learning how to be mortal."

"Is it common?"

"Used to be. Not anymore." Kael's expression hardened. "Most dragons won't risk it."

"Why not?"

"Because if one of you dies while bonded, the other could carry both magics. Fire and storm trying to exist in the same body." She met Allie's eyes. "I've seen it go two ways. Either the survivor burns out in days, torn apart from the inside, or they go mad when they lose the bond. Never ends well."

"Which is more common?"

Kael's silence was answer enough.

"So Erik and I…"

"Are linked until one of you breaks it or one of you dies." Kael picked up her blade again. "And breaking it while you're both alive will feel like its own kind of death."

The words hit harder than Allie expected. She swallowed and looked away, unable to breathe past the pressure in her chest.

Kael stood at last. "Read the book. I'll circle the block."

She left.

Alone, Allie set the book on the table. She opened the front cover.

Blank.

She flipped through more pages. Still blank.

Not empty. The paper felt weighted, as if words waited for the right reader.

She closed it again.

The duffel caught her eye. She reached for it, unzipped the top. Inside: flats, wrinkled clothes, the cardigan she had worn to court the day Mara died.

She dressed slowly, peeling off her rumpled shirt. The fabric dragged over sore skin.

She crouched again, searching. Lip balm. A comb. Something familiar.

Nothing. Just a flash drive and a crushed granola bar.

Frustrated, she turned back to the briefcase. Her fingers brushed the bottom.

Something thin. Papery.

She froze.

A matchbook.

Black paper. Silver lettering. *Dragon's Breath*. The same one she had picked up the night Mara died.

She opened the flap. The hand-drawn spiral was still there. But beneath it, something shimmered faintly. Lena's handwriting.

A number.

32.7401. -96.8282.

Coordinates.

She grabbed her phone. The GPS held. It dropped a pin in the West End. Old warehouses, condemned spaces. She zoomed in.

Near the edge of the pin, a name flickered: *Kors Custom Installations.*

The stairwell creaked.

Kael stepped inside. Allie held out the matchbook.

Kael took it. "Where'd you get this?"

"Back at the bar. The night Mara died. It was by the door."

Kael turned the matchbook over. "You know what *Dragon's Breath* is?"

"No."

"A band. From about ten years ago. Half dragons, half Watchers. They got too loud. Too reckless."

Her jaw tensed as her eyes landed on the scribbled numbers.

"You looked it up?"

Allie nodded. "It leads to a building. Kors's name is on it."

"Could be a trap."

"I don't care."

"You're not going alone."

"I figured."

"Ok, let's go."

Kael moved with practiced speed. She opened a few drawers, grabbing what she needed and stuffing it into her satchel. Picked up her sax and slung it over one shoulder. Then she waited for Allie, efficient, no wasted motion.

Allie changed. Flats for sneakers. Hair tied back. The pendant at her collarbone still pulsed faintly. Erik's presence remained, but he was far.

"I don't think he's coming back before we go," she said.

Kael buckled the last strap. "If he's smart, he won't follow."

"You think this is a bad idea?"

"Worse than that." Kael paused. "But you're right to go."

Kael handed her a folding knife. "Don't open this unless you mean it."

Allie weighed it. Heavy. Cold. Real.

"I was a lawyer a week ago."

"You still are."

They stood at the door. The wards pulsed once.

"We might not be able to come back," Kael said.

Allie looked around the room. The note still lay on the table. Her eyes moved to the box on the counter. She crossed the room, gathered it carefully, then slid it into the duffel with the book. She latched the briefcase and slung it over her shoulder.

"Just in case," she said quietly.

"You want to leave a note for him?"

Her hand brushed the table where Erik's handwriting marked the page. She thought of the dream. Of the fire and the storm.

Then she shook her head. "If he wants to find me, he will."

Kael gave a single nod. She opened the door.

Wind swept in, cold and sharp.

Allie stepped into it.

The safe-house closed behind them.

And the city opened wide.

CHAPTER 48

KAEL

The city thinned around them.

Skyscrapers gave way to rusted signage and cracked lots, businesses boarded shut. West Dallas looked like it had been left behind. Potholes ruled the streets. Neon flickered above hollow storefronts.

The rain had not stopped. It came down in sheets. Kael drove with both hands on the wheel, eyes fixed on the road.

Allie sat in silence beside her, watching water trail across the glass.

"You should eat something," Kael said.

Allie looked down. A half-crushed granola bar sat on the console. She peeled back the wrapper and chewed without tasting.

After a while, she said, "I saw Mara again. In the vision. I keep thinking if I'd been there, I could've stopped it."

Kael's expression softened. "You can't hold that."

"Why not? I'm the reason she was investigating the chain."

Kael drew a slow breath. "Magic doesn't care about guilt. It only listens to what we feed it."

The city slipped by in fragments. The coordinates on Allie's phone guided them closer to the river.

The rain softened to mist. The streets grew quiet. The red pin on the screen pulsed brighter.

Then the people vanished. The sidewalks went still.

Kael felt it first, a wrongness beneath the surface. She tightened her grip.

"That is the place," she said.

Through the streaked windshield, Allie saw the sign: Kors Custom Installations.

Her throat went dry. "I remember that name."

Kael opened her door. "Then let's see what it remembers about you."

The warehouse squatted at the edge of the block. Old brick layered with rusting steel panels. Windows fogged and sealed.

Too clean. Too untouched.

Kael held out a hand to stop her. "Wait."

She stepped forward alone, scanning the lot. No traffic. No sound but the rain on sheet metal.

She crouched and laid her fingers on the concrete near the entry. Warm.

Not just from the weather. Magic had moved through here recently.

She stood and turned back. "It's quiet. Too quiet."

"Meaning?"

"Meaning someone cleaned this place up."

The lock was already broken. Kael drew her blade and motioned for Allie to hold back. She lifted the metal enough to slip through.

The air inside was still, cooler than outside.

The floor was cracked concrete, dark with old stains. One corner held scattered tools, a steel basin, a drain. A half-folded cot rested in shadow. An oil drum burned low with greenish heat.

It felt lived in. Maintained.

Kael swept her light across the benches. Watcher grade sigil tools. Brass engraving rods, salt bowls, fractured containment crystals.

She turned toward the far wall. A tarp hung low. The shape beneath it was long and angular.

"Allie," she called.

The lawyer ducked under the door. The moment she stepped inside, her pendant pulsed.

"He's here," she whispered.

Kael peeled back the tarp.

The null bed sat there like a confession. Iron framed. Sigil lined. Inside it, a ward stone flickered blue.

"What is it?" Allie asked.

"A water-bind cradle. It keeps the dragon from shifting. Muffles the bond response. A cage for the mind."

Kael stepped closer and knelt. There, carved into the frame not with sigil tools but with a blade, was a name. Crude. Personal.

Morgan.

Kael stiffened. "I know that name."

A voice behind them said, "It was never meant to be found."

They both turned.

A man stood in the doorway. Tall and rain soaked. Silver hair slicked back. Eyes pale and deep.

William Kors.

This was not the man from photographs. This man filled the doorway. Quiet. Pressurized. And tired.

He stepped forward and shut the door behind him. "It's always colder when it's quiet. But it keeps the rage down."

Kael's hand slid closer to her blade.

"I wouldn't," William said gently. "Not here. Not while the bed's still warm."

Allie found her voice. "You're alive."

William looked at her, and for a moment his expression shifted. Recognition. Then pain.

"You're your mother's daughter," he said softly. "And your father's too."

His voice broke. He turned slightly, as if to hide it.

"I'm sorry," Allie whispered. "About Lena."

William closed his eyes. When he opened them again, they were wet.

"She died protecting you," he said. "Because I asked her to. Because she chose to."

The silence that followed was thick.

"What is this place?"

William exhaled. "This is the room where I don't become a monster. The room where I learned to survive losing everything."

He looked toward the cradle.

"I lost Morgan. Then your parents. Now Lena." His voice lowered. "She was all I had left."

Allie stepped forward. "You knew my parents."

"I did more than know them. They saved me once. From myself. From what I became after Morgan died."

He nodded toward the null bed.

"And when they were taken, I did what I could. I found you and Mara. I brought you both to Eleanor."

A tear slid down his cheek. He did not wipe it away. "Lena was supposed to outlive me."

"You've been watching me my whole life?"

He nodded. "Close enough to intervene. Far enough to avoid notice. Lena was closer. She kept you safe when I couldn't."

Kael's voice cut in. "Then why did she keep her sister's pendant? Why hide her things?"

William blinked. "Because I asked her to."

"Why?"

His voice turned raw. "Because we didn't know if the power would skip you. And if it did, then you deserved peace. If it didn't..."

He looked at Allie.

"Then every item tied to your sister was a lit match waiting for a fuse. Lena understood that. She carried that burden so you wouldn't have to."

CHAPTER 49

ALLIE

The words landed hard.

A lit match.

Her sister's pendant. The box. The book. The brooch. All of it, flame held inches from the edge.

Allie stared at William, and for the first time, she truly saw him.

The man who had carried two burning children from a house and vanished into a life of secrets.

The man who had left them in the care of someone who would not tell the whole story.

Allie swallowed. "You saved us, then stayed away. All these years, why?"

He looked toward the null cradle. The etched name. The worn stone. The years carved into it.

He turned back to her. "I wasn't safe. Not for anyone. Especially not for a child with storm in their blood."

The room went still.

Allie touched the pendant at her throat. "Lena gave me this right before she died."

William's breath caught. His eyes fixed on the pendant like it was a ghost.

He stepped closer, staring hard. "May I?"

She lifted it, letting the chain slide through her fingers. He did not touch it. He only looked.

William closed his eyes. Pain moved across his face like weather. "She wasn't supposed to. I told her to wait. I told her to give you time."

"Time for what?"

He opened his eyes again. Something cracked behind them. A truth too heavy to carry.

"That pendant isn't a suppressor, Allie. It's the opposite."

Her pulse stumbled. "I don't understand."

"The one Eleanor gave you after your parents died was meant to keep your magic dormant. To hide what you were. To keep the Watchers from sensing you." He gestured at the pendant. "But this one is older. Older than the curse itself."

Her hand closed around it. "Then what is it?"

William's voice turned reverent. "Your father's pen. Mara's pendant. The same object, different shapes."

"That's impossible."

"It's Serena's crown," he said. "From the first bond. The fern crown that blessed your bloodline. It changes form depending on who holds it. It becomes what its bearer needs most."

He looked at her with something close to awe. "Your father needed to disguise what he was. It became a pen. Mara needed to feel her power. It became a pendant."

"And me?"

"You needed to survive what was coming. So it stayed a pendant. A channel. A focus. Something that could keep you from burning your-self alive."

The pendant pulsed warm in her hand.

Allie stared at it. "I wore the wrong one."

"For three years you wore Eleanor's suppressor," William said softly. "You were normal because it held you down. Locked you away. But the night Lena died, when you touched your birthright, you woke up."

Her throat tightened. "What happens if I take it off?"

William's voice turned absolute. "You'd have full access to your power. No guidance. No control. If you used your powers without the pendant, you'd kill everyone in this room before you understood what you'd done."

"So I'm trapped."

"No. Not forever," William said. "You're protected. The crown knows what you can handle. It's teaching you. Slowly. When you're ready, it'll give you more."

"And the suppressor?" Allie asked. "The one I wore before."

"You don't need it," he said. "Keep it if you want, but you won't need it."

Allie pressed a hand to her chest. Her breath shook. "So Lena's death..."

"Woke you fully," William said. "Exactly the way Mara intended. Whether you were ready or not."

"Why now?" Allie asked. "Why the matchbook? Why leave something for me to find if it was all supposed to stay buried?"

"I didn't leave it. Or, if I did, I don't remember. Some days the shifts come faster than they used to. Sometimes I wake up in places I don't recognize, and things have been moved."

She saw it then.

The cracks behind his eyes.

The exhaustion beneath his calm.

Allie looked around the room. The press. The bed. The fraying wards. The ache behind her ribs.

The pendant glowed again. A flicker only she could see.

And for a moment, she saw something else too.

Lines of light cutting through the wards. A second pattern beneath the surface.

It vanished when she blinked.

Kael's hand brushed her arm. "You okay?"

"Yes." Allie stepped back. "We need to go."

But William stepped forward. "You should take this as well."

He opened a lower panel on the cradle. A small box rested inside, wrapped in a faded strip of blue silk.

Her mother's scarf.

Her breath stopped. She took the box with numb fingers.

Inside: a key. A strip of film. A photograph of Mara as a child holding a carved wooden dragon. And a folded piece of paper, stamped with a sigil she did not recognize.

"What is this?"

William's eyes drifted distant. "The last thing Lily gave me before she died."

"My mother?" Allie blinked rapidly. She wanted to know more, but William started to sway. The light flickered across the room.

Kael moved toward him. Her posture shifted. Concern edged into readiness. "William. Breathe. Your harness isn't lit."

"I know."

"You need to light it."

"I know." The word cracked.

The air in the workshop changed.

It thickened. Darkened. Water beaded on the pipes. The cradle hummed.

Kael grabbed his harness. The sigil resisted.

"Back," she ordered.

The cradle pulsed twice. Then cracked.

William dropped to one knee. Not in pain. In refusal.

"I won't go back in that bed," he said.

His voice was no longer entirely human.

Allie's pendant burned white-hot against her skin.

Kael yanked her backward.

Water exploded from the floor drain. Pipes split. Steam rose in a thick wave.

Then William roared.

The sound tore through the walls. It shook the stone. It shattered the cradle and split the cot in two.

Kael slammed her palm to the sigil lock. The metal screamed, then parted.

"Move," she shouted.

Allie ran.

CHAPTER 50

TORVALD

ar below the city, past forgotten tunnels and buried wards, the earth opened into a vault of black stone. The Hall of Five.

Torvald's boots struck the polished obsidian floor. His shadow stretched long behind him. The heat in the chamber was old and dry. The air smelled faintly of gold and ash.

Erik had stopped answering his calls. The boy was bonded now, caught in something deeper than duty, trying to find his footing on a path that no longer led back. Torvald had covered for him, invented reports, softened timelines.

But time was the enemy now.

Ahead, five thrones carved into the living rock stood in a semicircle. Each was inlaid with treasure: rubies, sapphires, gold laced through ancient sigils.

The Five waited.

They were old, older than any written record. Time had worn the illusion thin. Their eyes were too bright. Their stillness, too deep.

Councilor Ysra, eldest of them, leaned forward.

"Torvald. You have some explaining to do."

He inclined his head. "Then let us begin."

"You stand before us," said Councilor Maera, "because your rogue hunter has gone silent."

He bowed, but not deeply. "Varg is on assignment. He'll report when he's ready. I ask only for time."

"Or our patience," murmured Councilor Thorne from the shadow. His eyes gleamed silver-blue.

Councilor Idrin's voice was quieter, but no less sharp. "And what of Kael? What interest does your blood kin have in our missing hunter?"

Torvald's jaw flexed. "Kael is not rogue."

"And now," Maera added, "they run with a woman who has not been tested, not catalogued, not presented to this Council."

Torvald said nothing.

Thorne's voice sliced through the silence. "You will speak."

Torvald looked up, calm and cold. "You felt it."

They all had. The disturbance had cracked even the deepest shielding wards.

"I felt the earth shift," murmured Councilor Ansel. "I heard the song of old magic."

"You said she was dormant," Maera hissed. "You said she was harmless."

"I said she was unknown," Torvald replied. "There is a difference."

Councilor Idrin folded his hands. "And now she runs with your ghost of a hunter and a dragon with more scars than sense."

Torvald stepped forward, defiant. "And yet, none of them have drawn blood."

"Yet," Ysra said.

The space pressed against his lungs, thick and airless.

"You're afraid," he said quietly. "You should be. But fear has never been your ally."

"Neither has hubris," Thorne answered. "We remember what comes of unchecked bloodlines."

Torvald's gaze swept across them. "Then remember who stood beside you when it rose. Who held the line while the rest of you hid beneath this mountain."

Ansel's voice broke the silence. "The woman. Allie. What do you believe she is?"

Torvald answered without hesitation. "Something new."

Maera snarled. "That is not comforting."

"It is not meant to be."

The soul-flames guttered. Ysra stood slowly. Her robes swept the floor.

"We will not let this go unchecked. Erik has forty-eight hours to return to us with the girl, properly bound and presented. If he does not..."

"You will burn her," Torvald said. "You will send Retrieval."

"And you will not stop us," Thorne said. "Not this time."

Torvald gave a long breath. "If you send Retrieval, send a firebreak team with them."

Ysra's eyes narrowed. "Why?"

"Because if you corner them," he said, "you will not need a tribunal. You will need a battlefield."

None of them stopped him.

Not when war walked away from the table.

CHAPTER 51

ERIK

The rain had not stopped.

Erik pulled the collar of his coat higher as he climbed into his truck. Marcus's shop sat at the end of Riverside Drive, tucked between a closed fabrication plant and a storage facility.

Thorne Metalworks. The sign was hand-painted, fading.

The drive gave him time to think about the dream, about Allie's voice, about the heat and the way the bond had opened between them.

He told himself it was only a dream. He did not believe it.

The bond might demand connection. He would give it purpose instead. Protection. Distance. Anything but surrender.

He forced the thought away. He had a friend to find and too many dead to mourn.

The gates to Marcus's shop hung slightly open. That was wrong.

Marcus was cautious. Always. That gate was never left open.

He stopped the truck just outside. The air smelled off. Not blood. Not yet. But something close.

He stepped inside. The lights were low. The ward near the front desk flickered.

He moved through the foundry like a shadow.

He found Marcus near the main forge.

At first, it did not register. The body was too still.

Then he saw the blood.

It pooled beneath the stool. Streaked the front of Marcus's apron. His head tilted back, mouth slightly open, eyes gone blank.

Erik crossed the space in three strides. He knelt beside the body and pressed two fingers to the base of Marcus's throat.

The skin was cooling. The blood already drying.

But it was not just the death that stopped him. It was the mark.

A sigil had been burned into Marcus's chest. It glowed faintly, reacting to Erik's presence.

Morna's work.

The air near the forge still carried the weight of residual magic. The same flavor as what had surged from the safe-house.

Not Allie's. Not his. Hers.

He turned in a slow circle. Nothing had been ransacked. No struggle.

This was not a murder. It was a ritual.

By the vice clamp, something caught his eye. A scrap of paper. Folded.

Erik unfolded it. A single curl of blood made a shape across the page.

He stared at it. The scars along his forearm pulsed in response.

He refolded the paper and slipped it into his coat.

Five marks: Carlos, Milo, Mara, Lena, Marcus.

Fire. Earth. Storm. Water. Air. All accounted for.

One left. The sixth.

Not another element. The completion. The vessel.

No.

The bond pulsed beneath his ribs. Allie's heartbeat answered, quick and uneven.

He froze.

She was the sixth mark. She had always been the sixth.

The ritual did not need her dead. It needed her alive.

She was not the sacrifice. She was the gate.

He ran.

The drive was a blur. Rain hammered the windshield. The bond screamed warning.

But the bond still pulsed. She was alive. For now.

He abandoned the truck three blocks from the safe-house and ran. The wards flickered as he neared.

He burst inside. "Allie!"

Silence.

The main room was empty. Her briefcase sat on the table. Everything remained where she had left it.

The car keys were gone from the hook.

He crossed to the bedroom. The door stood open. Her coat was missing.

She was not here.

Erik pressed his palm to his chest. The bond pulsed beneath his ribs, steady but distant. She was not panicking. Not hurt. Just elsewhere.

He reached for her through the connection.

Allie?

A pause. Then her voice, faint but clear.

Erik? What's wrong?

Where are you?

Another pause. Suspicion colored the silence.

With Kael. We went to check something. Why?

Relief and fury collided in his chest.

You left without telling me.

I don't need your permission to leave.

The words stung. He exhaled slowly.

Are you coming back?

Yes. Soon. Is everything all right?

He could not tell her. Not like this.

Just get back here. Both of you.

Her presence faded. She had pulled away.

Erik paced the safe-house. Marcus's death replayed in flashes. The sigil. The blood.

Five marks complete. One left.

Allie was the sixth. The vessel. The gate.

The sound of the door opening snapped him back.

Allie stepped inside first, rain dripping from her hair, Kael close behind.

Allie's gaze found his immediately. "What happened?"

Erik pointed at her. "Bathroom. Now."

Kael lifted a brow but stayed silent.

Allie frowned. "Excuse me?"

"Now."

Something in his voice, quiet and commanding, made her move. She crossed the room without another word. Erik followed, closing the door behind them with a soft click.

The space was small. Too small. He could smell the rain on her skin, the sharp trace of her shampoo, the heat radiating off her body.

"What's going on?" she asked, arms crossed.

"We need to talk about last night." His voice came low, steady but frayed at the edges. "The dream."

Her expression shuttered. "What about it?"

"It didn't mean anything. The bond made us…"

"I know what the bond did."

"So we agree. This stays professional."

"Fine." Her tone could have frozen steel.

He should have stopped there. But the words tangled. "I'm not saying it wasn't real. I'm saying it can't happen. Not again. You didn't choose this. Neither did I. And I won't…"

"Won't what?" she snapped. "Won't let me decide what I want? Won't risk losing control?"

"That's not what I…"

"Then what are you saying?"

"I'm saying the bond is dangerous. My parents…"

"I don't care about your parents." The anger cracked into something rawer. "I care about you deciding what I can handle," Allie said, stepping back. The pendant flared.

Erik's eyes widened. "Allie…" The lights flickered.

The scars on his chest pulsed once, hard, like something had pulled it. She felt it too. A snap of connection, there and gone.

"What was that?" she breathed.

Erik touched his chest, frowning. "I don't know. The bond shouldn't... react like that."

They stared at each other in the suddenly quiet room.

"Has that happened before?" Allie asked.

"No." He looked at her differently now. "Never."

His hand rose before he could stop it, catching her wrist before she touched his scars.

"I brought you in here because I didn't want an audience. Kael's air hears everything."

She tried to pull away. He did not let go.

Her face tipped up toward his. Eyes dragon-bright. Still furious and curious. Her breath hitched. His gaze dropped to her mouth.

Error. He knew it. Still, he did not back away.

Allie froze. His touch burned. Every nerve lit, dragging her toward him when she should have pulled away.

He did not.

"The air hears everything," he said again, quieter this time.

Her breath brushed his skin. The bond trembled, waiting.

Then he moved. His hand slipped to her waist, pulling her in one sharp motion. Her gasp hit his mouth and became something else entirely.

The kiss landed hard, heat and defiance, control unraveling in one heartbeat.

Her hands found his coat, fisting the fabric like she meant to test every boundary he had just set. The bond flared, gold light threading through the cracks in his restraint. For one reckless second, he let it burn.

Her back hit the wall. His hands framed her face. The sound she made undid him.

Then she shoved him back. Hard.

He caught himself on the sink, chest heaving. For a second, neither moved. The bond thrummed between them, gold light fading to ember. His scars glowed faint beneath his sleeves, pulse for pulse with hers.

"No."

He blinked. "Allie…"

"No." Her tone cut clean through the air. "You just gave the stay professional speech." She waved a hand between them, quick and sharp. "So no to this."

"I know what I said."

"Then stick to it, Erik."

He exhaled, dragging a hand through his hair. The silence buzzed between them, heavy with everything they had not stopped.

"Fine," he said at last. "Your choice. For now."

Her eyes narrowed. "For now?"

He met her gaze, unflinching. "If you want to turn a dragon off, go for the ego. Tell me my scars make you sick. That you hate tall men. That I smell like smoke and bad choices." His voice dropped lower. "But no? That's just a challenge."

The air went still. Her pulse jumped, betraying her.

"You're impossible."

"Dragon-born, sweetheart. Comes with the territory."

Her mouth twitched despite herself. For half a heartbeat the fight left her eyes, then it snapped back.

"Are we done?"

"Not even close." He straightened, the heat between them fading into something colder. "Marcus is dead."

The words hit like a physical blow. Allie's breath caught. "What?"

"I found him an hour ago. Murdered. Same sigil as the others."

"Five marks," she whispered.

"Five elements," Erik corrected. "Fire. Earth. Storm. Water. Air. All accounted for."

Her hand moved to her chest, fingers brushing the pendant. "One more to go."

"I don't think so." His voice was quiet. Certain. "There's one more mark, yes. The sixth."

"But you just said…"

"Five elements. One vessel." He looked at her, and the weight of it settled between them like stone. "You're the sixth mark, Allie. You always were."

Her face went pale.

"The ritual doesn't need you dead," he continued. "It needs you alive. You absorbed the power when the sigil imploded. You're not the sacrifice. You're the gate."

She took a step back, her shoulders hitting the wall. "No."

"The killer isn't hunting you to finish the pattern. She's hunting you to complete it. Through you."

Allie's breathing quickened. The pendant at her throat pulsed brighter, reacting to her fear.

"I'll do everything I can to protect you," he said softly. "You must know that."

"Yes," she said slowly. "We need to tell Kael."

"We will."

She nodded once, then pushed past him toward the door.

"Allie." His voice stopped her.

She paused, hand on the doorknob, but did not turn.

"I meant what I said. About protecting you."

"I know."

"And I meant what I said about the rest of it too."

She looked back at him then, her expression unreadable. "Which part?"

"All of it."

She pulled the door open and stepped through.

Kael was waiting in the main room, leaning against the desk with her arms crossed. Her gaze flicked between them, sharp and assessing.

"Have a nice chat?" she asked, her tone dry.

Neither of them answered.

Erik stepped past Allie, his voice flat. "Marcus is dead. Fifth element complete. Allie is the sixth mark."

Kael's expression went cold. "I know. I heard."

Outside, thunder rolled low through the city, patient and waiting.

CHAPTER 52

ALLIE

The safe-house was quiet. The lanterns hummed low. Pipes ticked in the walls.

Allie stood in the doorway for a moment, letting her eyes adjust. The room still held the echo of raised voices from the bathroom.

Kael had angled a metal chair toward the door and sat with her arms folded. Erik paced once along the far wall, turned, and stopped.

Kael's gaze flicked to Allie's face, then to Erik, then back. "Talk," she said.

Allie pulled out the chair and sat. She laced her fingers together to keep them from shaking.

"All right," she said. Her voice was steadier than she felt. "Let's start with what we know."

She laid it out the way she would in court.

"Five dragons are dead. Including my sister and my best friend. Each tied to a different element. Each one marked by an elemental sigil. Marcus makes five. That leaves one." She paused. "Me."

The corner of Kael's mouth twitched. Erik said nothing.

Allie hesitated, then added, quieter, "And who is Elena?"

That name changed the room.

Even Kael went still.

217

Erik's expression did not shift much, but something beneath it cracked. His scars pulsed faintly under his sleeves. He did not speak.

Kael moved quickly. She crossed to the table and picked up her saxophone, fingers tapping across the wind-stone. Tense, but still. She leaned back against the wall.

"Erik?" she said.

He rubbed the back of his neck. When he finally spoke, his voice was quiet and measured.

"Elena," he said slowly. "It has to be Elena Mendez."

Allie straightened. "Who is she?"

He met her eyes. "Alliance. The only living storm-born we know of. Her son was Carlos."

"The third death," Allie said quietly.

Erik nodded once.

"My mother knew her. They were friends. When Carlos died, Elena called. Asked her to send me to investigate. I thought she was grieving."

He did not say the rest, but Allie saw it in his face.

You thought wrong.

"She brought you in for a reason," Allie said carefully. "You think she knew?"

Erik did not answer right away.

"There's more," he said finally. "The vision. The one we shared."

He looked at her. The bond between them pulsed.

"The woman in the glen, it was her."

Allie froze. "That was Elena? The storm-born casting the sigil?"

"She was younger. But the magic was the same. So was the grief."

Allie nodded slowly. "I saw her too. She was with a man, fire-born. That must've been her husband. Her bonded."

"She tried to break the curse," Erik said. "She and Jacob. Storm and fire."

"And she failed," Allie whispered. "It killed him. Tore the bond apart."

Kael's arms tightened across her chest. "And left her with the fallout."

Erik nodded. "She survived. No one else ever has."

Allie sat back. "She's not the killer. She cannot be. Her son…"

"She might not be," Kael said cautiously. "But she's connected. Deeply. That vision wasn't a warning. It was history."

Kael's fingers tightened on the sax. "And now she's resurfaced for a reason. I saw her watching the safe-house this morning."

Allie went still. "You saw her?"

Kael nodded once. "Across the street. She didn't hide."

Erik swore under his breath. "She knows where we are."

Allie's pulse stumbled. "Then she wanted us to know."

She looked at Erik. "Do you think she's trying to help?"

"I don't know," he admitted. "But she's the only one who has ever seen a bond collapse from the inside. She lived through it. If anyone knows what this ritual is, it's her."

Kael's voice was dry. "Or she knows how to finish it."

Allie did not answer right away. The pendant against her chest pulsed once.

"Either way," she said, "we need to talk to her."

Erik met her eyes. "Then we find her."

Kael did not move. But she did not argue.

The three of them sat in silence.

Outside, the rain began to fall harder.

CHAPTER 53

ERIK

The storm had passed.

The air still felt charged, as if something unseen lingered in the corners of the room, listening.

Erik stood by the desk, arms folded. Kael sat with her feet hooked on the edge of the table, flicking her wind-stone into the air and catching it. Allie leaned over the map they had pieced together, brow furrowed in concentration.

They were close. But not close enough.

Erik reached for his cell and tapped connect.

The line rang twice. Torvald answered on the third.

"Where are you?"

Clipped. Irritated. Someone speaking under pressure.

"They want answers," Torvald said. "Status. Timeline. Whether she's stable."

Erik's voice stayed steady. "They'll have to wait."

A pause. Hard and flat.

"I need to speak with someone," Erik said. "Elena Mendez."

Another pause followed, heavier. A weighted silence, like someone had stepped into the room behind Torvald.

"Why?"

"She's connected," Erik said. "The vision Allie and I shared. It was her. Younger. Before the collapse. Before Jacob."

Across the table, Kael's wind-stone dropped silently into her palm. Allie did not move, but her shoulders tightened, the bond flickering with unease.

A sharp breath crackled through the line.

"You're sharing visions now?"

He hesitated. "We are."

Torvald exhaled through his teeth. "That's not normal, Erik. Not even for a bond."

"I know."

"And you're certain it was Elena?"

"I am."

"She's not part of this investigation."

"She is now," Erik said. "Five marks are down. The sixth is about to fall. She might know what comes next."

Torvald did not speak at first. Erik could almost hear him pacing, weighing risks, choosing which rules he was willing to break.

At last, Torvald said, "She still owns property near the north wall. Edge of the city. Quiet stretch. No neighbors. She goes there when she wants to be forgotten."

"Good," Erik said. "We'll…"

"No."

Erik's expression hardened. "You don't trust me?"

"I don't trust her," Torvald replied. Then, softer, "And I trust what this bond's doing to you even less."

Erik said nothing.

Torvald gave the address anyway. A stretch of road just past the outer wall. Then, as if forced to speak it aloud:

"Ashvale Glen."

The name struck like a blow.

He had seen it before. Not in memory. In the shared vision. A

222

street sign blurred by storm-light, just before the collapse. He had not understood it then.

Now he did.

The line clicked dead.

Erik lowered the comm slowly.

"What?" Allie asked. Her voice was quiet, but she had felt it, the shift in him, the pulse tightening through the bond.

He looked at her. "In the vision, did you see a street sign?"

Her brow furrowed. "Yes. But it blurred. I couldn't read it."

"Ashvale Glen," Erik said. His gaze held hers.

Her breath hitched.

Recognition. Unease.

He reached across the table, found the street on the map, and marked it.

Allie stepped forward. Her gaze followed his hand, then widened. "Erik..."

She did not need to say more.

The other five points, Marcus, Lena, Ash, Carlos, and the alley, circled inward on the paper.

And this, Ashvale Glen. The sixth. The final mark.

A pattern. A sigil. A ritual carved through the city.

Not imagined. Not coincidence. Real.

"We're not guessing anymore," Erik said.

Allie's hand flattened on the map, right over Ashvale Glen. Fear flickered through her, but resolve rose faster.

"Then we go to her," she said. Her voice was steady. Certain. "We don't wait for the sixth mark to fall. We go now. We end this."

Kael's eyes flicked to her, then to Erik. "You're sure?"

"Something wants me there," Allie said. "So I'll go."

Erik met her gaze. The bond pulsed between them, a quiet promise.

"Together," he said.

"Together," she agreed.

Kael stood. Her expression unreadable, but her posture steady. She nodded once. "Then let's move."

Erik glanced toward the door as the wind shifted.

"Someone's waiting," he murmured.

He did not say who.

He did not need to.

The bond already knew.

CHAPTER 54

ELENA

The storm had washed the ash from the windows.

Elena sat by the fire she had not lit. It burned anyway. The sigil carved into the hearthstone refused to sleep. Its light crawled up her wrists.

Outside, the rain had quieted to a whisper. She could feel them through it. The girl, the dragon, the windbound soldier.

They were close now.

Closer than she had planned.

She pressed her palms together, felt the cracks in her skin. The bond had not killed her. It had left her unfinished.

"Jacob," she whispered. "They found the sixth."

The flames guttered once.

Elena looked toward the door. The wards shivered.

They were coming.

CHAPTER 55

WILLIAM

The rain had stopped, but the world still dripped.

Water ran through the cracks in the concrete floor, thin silver threads weaving around the shattered cradle. The air smelled of ash and iron.

William sat where the girls had left him. The fire had gone out hours ago, but something still clung to the edges of things, not fire, not magic, only the memory of both.

His hands shook when he tried to move them. The sigils burned out along his forearms glowed a dull blue, the color of exhaustion.

He could not remember what he had said last. Only that Allie had looked at him the same way her mother, Lily, once had.

Soft eyes. Hard truth.

A dragon recognizing another.

He laughed once. The sound cracked halfway.

"Too young," he whispered. "Too young for any of this."

The forge answered with a hiss. Steam coiled from a crack near the drain.

Water spoke there sometimes. He had learned to listen.

Not words. Not really. More like sound that remembered shape.

Tonight it said her name.

Eleanor.

He froze.

The whisper came again, through the pipe beneath the floor, urgent now. The water carried something else too, the sharp current of fear.

"Eleanor," he repeated. "You're in trouble."

He rose unsteadily. The water in his blood stuttered, then caught. The sigils along his skin flared, responding to a will he barely remembered owning.

He did not remember leaving the workshop. Only the rain.

The streets blurred. Lights bled into water. The city leaned and tilted around him like a ship half-sunk. He followed the pull of the whisper, the drag of water through the gutters, until the street signs began to make sense again.

Eleanor's house waited at the end of the block, half-hidden by an oak that had been growing since before Dallas had a name. The porch light burned dim yellow through the fog.

He hesitated at the gate. Something was wrong. The air shimmered faintly, too still, too symmetrical. He reached toward it and felt the hum of containment magic, fine as spider silk and twice as cruel.

Watchers.

He stepped through anyway.

The ward snapped like ice underfoot. The sound cracked the silence.

Eleanor opened the door before he could knock. Her hair was loose around her shoulders, and her eyes widened when she saw him.

"William," she said softly. "What are you doing here?"

He opened his mouth, but the words would not line up. His thoughts splintered in all directions. The message the water had carried tangled in his mind.

"They're coming," he managed. "You have to…"

The ward flared behind him.

Light broke across the yard.

Three Watchers stepped through the shimmer, masks gleaming

228

silver in the rain. Their robes caught the wind like wings. Eleanor raised a hand, already forming a counter-sigil, but she was too late.

The first strike hit the ground beside her, sending a pulse of energy through the porch. Wood splintered. The doorframe cracked. William threw himself between her and the second blast, his back taking the brunt of it.

The water inside him tried to answer, but it sputtered, wild and broken. It had been too long since he had called on it fully. The power came out in bursts, unfocused and fierce, a dragon's breath turned to ruin.

He roared once, and the air turned white.

The nearest Watcher fell. The other two advanced.

"Run," he shouted.

Eleanor did not move. "I won't leave you."

He turned toward her. The sight blurred. For an instant, she was not Eleanor but someone else, someone with storm-light in her hair and the scent of smoke on her skin.

"Morgan," he whispered. "No. Not again."

The third strike hit him square in the chest.

The world tilted sideways. The sound of the rain returned all at once, loud and endless. He landed on the steps, his shoulder catching the edge of a broken post. His lungs burned. The sigils on his arms dimmed to embers.

Through the blur, he saw Eleanor fall. Her spell broke in her hands, light scattering across the yard like dust. One of the Watchers caught her before she hit the ground. Another gathered the pieces of the shattered ward into a containment sigil.

They dragged her toward the car waiting at the curb.

"Stop," William tried to say. The word came out as smoke.

He reached for dragon power. Found only water.

The rain poured over his face, cold and constant. Somewhere beneath it, the whisper began again, soft and mournful.

He tried to stand. His legs did not obey.

Eleanor's head lifted once as they pulled her away. Their eyes met across the distance.

She mouthed something he could not hear.

Then the car door closed.

The lights faded down the street until only the sound of rain remained.

William sank to the ground beside the broken porch. The water inside him surged.

He pressed his hand against the wet concrete, feeling the faint heartbeat of water beneath it.

"Tell them," he whispered. "Tell them where she's gone."

The water pulsed once in answer.

Then it was still.

CHAPTER 56

ELEANOR

The rain had softened by evening.

Inside, Eleanor stood barefoot in the kitchen, rinsing her tea mug. The kettle hissed softly behind her.

Allie had called that morning. Apologetic, breathless.

"Something came up. I'll come this weekend, I promise."

Eleanor had believed her. She was also relieved that Allie had stayed away. It was safer that way.

The Watchers had not followed up since the night Mara died. They had vanished after Allie failed to appear. Said they would find her on their own. Said she was a danger now.

Eleanor knew what that meant. Erasure. Still, they had left her alone. For now.

She poured the water and stirred the tea slowly. For a few hours, she had allowed herself to believe it was over.

She had just crossed to the cabinet when the wind chime outside stirred once. No breeze followed. Just the faint ring of metal.

Her hand stilled.

The doorbell did not ring. The wards did.

A shimmer cut across the windows. Containment magic. That meant Watchers.

Then came a knock. Not on the door. On the wards themselves. It shattered the spell.

She turned toward the front hall and opened the door.

William stood there. Soaked, eyes wide.

"William," she said, her breath catching. "What are you doing here?"

He opened his mouth. "They're coming. You have to…"

The wards flared behind him. Light broke across the yard.

Three Watchers stepped through the shimmer, masks gleaming silver in the rain. Their robes caught the wind like wings. Eleanor raised a hand, already forming a counter-sigil, but she was too late.

The first strike hit the ground beside her, sending a pulse of energy through the porch. Wood splintered. The doorframe cracked.

William threw himself between her and the second blast. His back took the brunt of it. The magic in the air swelled. Hungry. Wrong.

She shouted, "This is unlawful…"

But the spell struck. A pulse of force hit her ribs. She fell hard.

William roared. The air turned white. One Watcher dropped. The other two advanced.

"Run," he shouted.

Eleanor did not move. "I won't leave you." She tried to rise. Her spell flickered, half-formed.

Then William went still. The third strike hit him in the chest. He folded, fire vanishing from his eyes.

Something inside Eleanor cracked. She screamed.

But the last Watcher reached her first. Hands seized her arms. A containment band snapped around her wrist. Her body went limp. Magic severed.

"Will," she tried to say.

His eyes flickered open once. Their gazes met. She mouthed one word.

Run.

Then the car door slammed shut.

* * *

THE LIGHT RETURNED IN PIECES. Stone beneath her cheek. A cold pulse against her temple. Damp air that smelled of rust and ash.

She opened her eyes.

The ceiling above her was concrete. Cracked. Old water lines crossed it. No windows. Only a single flickering lantern.

Eleanor shifted. Her hands would not move.

She looked down and saw fine black threads wrapping her wrists, binding her to an iron ring bolted to the floor.

Not Watcher work. Too elegant. Too old.

She sat up slowly. Pain followed.

"Don't pull on the binding," said a voice from the dark. "It bites."

Eleanor froze.

The voice belonged to a girl. No older than Allie. Perhaps younger. Smooth. Calm.

Then the girl stepped into the light.

She wore white. A simple dress. Her bare feet made no sound. Her hair was too dark for her skin. Her eyes were too still for her age.

She smiled like someone who had never once meant it.

"You're awake," she said.

Eleanor swallowed. Her voice came out rough. "Where am I?"

"You're somewhere you can't get out of."

The girl crouched beside her.

"But not for long. We only need you until she comes."

Eleanor stared at her. "Who?"

The girl tilted her head, smile widening. "Allie, of course."

A chill crept over Eleanor's skin. "Why?"

"She's the last. The storm. The sixth of the wheel."

The girl's voice softened.

"And you're her kin. She'll come if we call with the right voice."

Eleanor tried to summon magic, but the weave was too tight. It was not just binding her arms. It was muffling her power.

For most of her life, to the outside world, she had only been a Watcher. Scholar. Memory-keeper. Not a practitioner. But that had never been true.

Watchers were witches. The oldest kind. Sigils and blood. A legacy of power kept quiet by design. It was burning now. The threads of it still hummed beneath her skin, furious and tangled.

"You don't have to do this," she said. "Whatever you think you are creating…"

"Creating?" The girl laughed. "No, Eleanor. This has always been. And it's almost ready."

She stood. Her gaze drifted toward the far wall, where a sigil glowed faintly. Not red. Not gold. Something older.

"She was always going to come," the girl said softly. "We just made sure she had a reason."

Eleanor's pulse kicked. "You're not Watchers," she whispered.

"No."

The girl's smile vanished.

"They were too slow. Too blind. We're here to finish what the old ones started."

Eleanor flinched. "Who are you?"

But the girl did not answer. She was already walking away.

Before she closed the door, she whispered,

"Morna's kin."

The door slid shut. And Eleanor was alone.

* * *

THE SILENCE PRESSED IN. Morna. The name echoed in Eleanor's blood. It had been buried for decades, erased by the Watchers so thoroughly that most could not even say who she was anymore.

But Eleanor remembered.

Morna had stood at the edge of the world with a storm at her back and grief in her hands. And she had tried to end everything.

To hear that name now meant only one thing.

This was not about Allie's power. This was about her lineage.

Eleanor's hands trembled against the binding thread.

This was not vengeance. This was legacy.

Only the sigil pulsed now. Slow. Patient. Counting down.

CHAPTER 57

KILLER - MOIRA

The corridors beneath the city were quiet.

Moira walked without hurry, her bare feet silent on the old tile. She passed beneath a row of rusted pipes and veered right, deeper into the vault.

The light here was different. Soft, but wrong. Magic bled into the walls in places. It left the air tasting faintly of ash.

At the end of the hall, a sigil glowed above the threshold. Pale blue. Contained. Sealed.

She stepped through.

The containment chamber was clean. Sparse. Only one lantern burned high in the corner. The captive, Eleanor Vance, lay curled on the stone floor nearby. Still bound, but awake now. Watching.

That pleased her.

Moira crossed the room slowly. She crouched beside Eleanor.

"You're a gift," she said.

Eleanor did not answer.

"You kept secrets for years. Protected things you barely understood." Moira stood. "But delay costs lives."

Still, Eleanor said nothing.

Moira walked the perimeter, one hand trailing along the wall.

"She'll come. You know she will. That's why you're here."

Eleanor flinched.

Moira's smile deepened.

"You remember what they said about Morna?"

The name landed heavy.

Eleanor's voice rasped. "She's gone."

Moira turned back to her, gaze steady. "The blood remembers. And your little niece is the key."

She knelt again. "Did you think the storm would rise without a reckoning?"

Eleanor whispered, "You'll kill her."

"No," Moira said. "We'll complete her."

She stood slowly.

"You always misunderstood the ritual. You thought it was death."

She smiled.

"It is rebirth."

CHAPTER 58

ELENA

The chamber breathed.

Elena stepped into the circle and felt it answer. The stone beneath her boots pulsed. Light from the upper vents slanted through the dust. Six sigils already burned. One remained untouched.

She walked the circumference slowly, her hand trailing the grooves. Every mark hummed with stored power. Every death had been a promise kept.

The first for earth. The second for storm. The third for flame reborn.

Her son.

Elena stopped at that sigil and let her fingers hover above it. The lines were darker here, cut deeper. Carlos had been the fulcrum. The strongest magic had to come from her own blood. When the light had faded from his eyes, the rush had risen to take its place.

It had never left her.

She straightened and moved on. The fourth sigil still smoked faintly. The fifth shimmered with cold. The sixth waited, half-drawn, empty and hungry.

The storm's mark. Allie's.

Elena looked up toward the vaulted ceiling. Beyond it, the sky churned. The storm was gathering, just as the texts had promised. When the girl stepped into the circle, the elements would converge. The curse would fold in on itself. Morna would claim her vessel.

Behind her, footsteps whispered across the tile.

Moira entered, barefoot in a white dress. The backlash from the sigil rupture had twisted something in her, left magic stitched wrong beneath her skin.

Elena watched her closely. The madness had quieted, but it had not left.

Elena stepped closer. "Are you ready?"

Moira's smile widened. "I'm the echo. The edge. I was born ready."

Elena nodded. "Good."

Moira tilted her head. "She's close. The air's changing."

The circle pulsed under their feet. A ripple shivered through the wards above.

Elena felt it too. The old protections had stirred once, then gone still.

Visitors.

"Elena," Moira said again. "Did you feel it?"

"I did." Elena's fingers rested on the basin. "They're here."

Moira's eyes glittered. "The storm and the flame."

From the shadows beyond the circle, the old Watchers stood waiting. Not the modern enforcers, but those who had lived long enough to forget their names. Time-worn. Pale-eyed. They had come to witness.

Elena did not speak to them. Their presence was a seal.

She faced the center again. "Is the bait secured?"

"She is."

"Good," Elena said. "Then everything's ready."

"Six lives for one soul," Moira murmured, almost smiling. "And the world gets a goddess in return."

Elena answered with a faint smile. "A fair trade."

The storm above them flared once.

Earth. Storm. Fire. Water. Air.

The five answered. One still called.

For a heartbeat, she saw the girl's face. Her son's eyes. Her husband's fire. The shape of a family she had tried to rebuild from ash.

The thought burned, then passed.

When it was done, the curse would break. The bond would restore.

She had already lost everything that mattered.

This was not loss. This was completion.

CHAPTER 59

ALLIE

The truck rumbled beneath them as Erik guided it down the narrow road. The safe house shrank in the side mirror.

Allie sat in the passenger seat, arms crossed tight. Her pendant pulsed once against her throat, faint and warm.

"Is it supposed to do that?" she asked quietly.

Erik did not glance over. "Do what?"

"The pendant. It's been glowing since we left."

"It does."

She frowned. "But what's it doing?"

"It's tied to your bond. And to mine. And Kael's too. It responds to dragon-kind. It activates when the circle draws close."

Allie looked down at it. "Can everyone see it?"

"Only those who can feel it," Erik said. "Humans without bond-blood won't register it as anything more than glass."

She shifted in her seat. "It never glowed around me before."

"Because it wasn't active. Or you weren't ready."

She was quiet for a moment. "So, what now?"

He tapped the wheel once. "Now you learn. Slowly."

"You mean until someone tries to use me as a vessel again."

"Okay," he said, glancing at her. "Low pressure."

She snorted despite herself.

They sat in silence. The city hummed below them.

"How do you know what you feel is real?" Allie asked finally.

Erik was quiet for a moment. "You think the bond's controlling us."

"I think the bond makes us feel things we might not otherwise feel. And I don't know how to separate what's magic and what's..." She trailed off.

"What's real," he finished.

"Yeah."

More silence passed between them.

"I could tell you the bond doesn't work that way," Erik said. "That it only amplifies what's already there. That it's about recognition, not creation."

"But I wouldn't believe you."

"No. You wouldn't."

She finally looked at him. "So what do we do?"

"We survive tomorrow. And then we figure out what's left."

"And if nothing's left?"

"Then we walk away." He met her eyes. "No bond. No obligation. Just choice. Neither of us asked for this. I didn't want it either."

"You'd let me go."

"It'd be hard. Especially if the bond can't be broken. But yes."

Something in her chest eased. Not the bond. Something smaller. More human. The fear that she was trapped.

"You're not what I expected," she said quietly.

"What did you expect?"

"Someone more... possessive. Someone who'd use the bond as leverage. As proof we're meant to be together."

Erik shook his head. "The bond's proof we can be together. Not that we should be. That's up to you. To us. To choice."

Allie looked out over the city. "You've had a lot of time to get good at letting people go, haven't you?"

"Too much time," Erik admitted. "I've learned that nothing lasts unless both people choose it. Every day. Even with magic binding them together."

"Is that what you want? For me to choose you?"

"I want you to choose yourself first," he said. "Whatever that means."

She studied his face in the dim light. Centuries of loss etched into the lines around his eyes. He meant it. He would walk away if that was what she needed.

And somehow, knowing that made her want to stay.

"Okay," she said.

"Okay?"

"After we survive tomorrow. After the dust settles. We'll figure out what's real."

Erik nodded. "Deal."

They sat in silence. After a moment, Allie's hand found his. Not the bond pulling them together. Just two people choosing, in that moment, not to be alone.

"For what it's worth," she said quietly, "I think I'd probably like you even without magic forcing the issue."

His mouth curved. "Probably?"

"Don't push your luck, grandpa."

He laughed. The sound surprised them both.

Tomorrow they would face a curse, and a resurrection, and a battle neither was certain they would survive.

But tonight, in a truck on the way to face their fate, they were just two people who might be falling for each other.

Or might just be falling.

Time would tell.

Kael had peeled off from the safe house ahead of them, vanishing into the rising wind with a wordless nod. Now, as they neared the street, the air felt tighter. Charged.

They turned a corner. The lights ahead dimmed.

Torvald was already there, leaning against a rusted lamppost, arms folded. His coat hung open. Kael stood beside him, silent, her hair loose and wind-bitten.

The truck groaned to a stop. Allie opened the door.

Her sneakers hit the curb.

Rain misted in the air, but it was not falling. It hovered.

Erik nodded once. Torvald returned it. No words. Just old loyalty.

Kael looked over. "You ready for this?"

"No," Allie said honestly.

Torvald grunted once. "Then you're sane."

They fell in step together. Four figures beneath a flickering street sign.

The name stretched across it in faded white letters: *Ashvale Glen*.

The paint was sun-worn and peeling. Just old.

Allie stared up at it.

She had seen that name once before. Not on a map. Not in a file. But in the vision she and Erik had shared, the day the pendant first lit and her storm cracked the ground open.

A sign. A warning.

It had been fuzzy then. Edges blurred.

But now the sight was clear. Real. Solid. Waiting.

She looked at the others. Their faces were calm. Resolved.

Her pendant flared again.

They moved forward.

Toward the beginning of the end.

CHAPTER 60

KAEL

The wind met her at the door.

Kael stepped into it without hesitation, letting the weight of the safe house fall away behind her. She left Erik and Allie without pause. There were times for walking beside someone, and times for walking ahead.

The others would follow by road. But Kael was wind-born.

She closed her eyes and let the current rise. Her breath caught once, then released. The wind whispered with force. A stillness just before movement.

Then she vanished.

Not gone. Just between things.

The wind carried her through the city. Over streets littered with old wards and damp leaves. Past corners she remembered only in fragments. Power still clung to the bones of the protections Erik had laid, enough to slow pursuit but not enough to hold if violence came.

A sharp turn took her north. She kept to the shadows, the current guiding her.

When the streets narrowed, her thoughts narrowed with them. Memory rose where she did not want it to. Torvald's voice, colder than the rain. His disapproval. His duty. His absence.

They had spoken the night before. The distance between them had only widened. No apology. No grief. Just another lecture from a man too loyal to rules to mourn the girl he failed.

When Mara died, he had not come to the funeral. He had sent a single rose. Cold. Precise. Duty-bound.

She had hated him for that.

He had once told her, *You carry the last of the line. Do not forget your place in it.*

She had not forgotten. She had simply stopped caring.

It did not take long to reach the edge.

Ashvale Glen.

Kael slowed just before the corner. Let her feet touch pavement. Let the wind settle.

Torvald was already there.

He stood beneath the street sign, arms crossed, shoulders unmoving. Only his eyes shifted, tracking her approach.

"Little loud for a ghost," he said without looking directly at her.

Kael smiled faintly. "And you're a little early for the end."

"I like to be prepared."

He almost smiled, but it never reached his eyes. He glanced at her briefly.

"You cut your hair again."

"I sever what weighs me down."

He nodded once. "Including your future."

She stepped closer, voice low. "Spit it out, Torvald. I'm not in the mood for quiet judgment."

"You're meant to carry forward. That's all."

She snorted. "Then find someone else to build your dynasty. My name's not a cradle."

Silence stretched between them. Their breath fogged the air.

He spoke first. "You never forgave me for Mara."

"You never asked for forgiveness." Kael's voice chilled. "You sent a rose to her funeral. A rose. As if she were a contract that expired."

"I did what was required."

"Required by whom? The Alliance? Your pride?" Her voice

cracked, sharp as a pressure snap. "Or was it required by whatever made you so afraid of caring that you forgot how."

Torvald's jaw tightened. His gaze moved across her face. Really moved. For perhaps the first time in years.

The wind rose between them, catching her hair, snapping his coat.

"Kael," he said quietly. "I didn't stay away because I didn't care."

"Then why."

He hesitated. The silence behind it was old.

"Because caring for you would've made you vulnerable. And I don't know how to protect anything I care about anymore."

Kael froze.

It was the closest thing to an apology he had ever given.

He reached slowly into his coat and pulled out something small. A photograph.

Mara and Kael, laughing, saxophone in hand, the night she graduated from the Academy.

"I kept this," he said. "I shouldn't have. But I did."

Her throat tightened. She took it with trembling fingers.

"I'm sorry," Torvald said. And this time, he meant it.

The wind softened around them.

Kael slipped the photograph into her jacket pocket, over her heart.

"All right," she said. "Then here's my answer."

He waited.

"I'll protect Allie. With or without the Alliance. I won't lose another storm-born."

His eyes closed, briefly, painfully. "Then I won't stand in your way."

The wind rose around them in a slow spiral.

"They're close," Kael murmured.

Torvald nodded. "Good. I'm tired of waiting."

Headlights appeared through the mist, climbing the curve of the road.

Some bridges could not be rebuilt.

But some wounds could begin to heal.

Kael lifted her face to the storm, the photograph warm beneath her coat.

"Let's finish this," she said.

Together, uncle and niece turned toward the headlights as the others arrived.

The Wind-born line was no longer divided.

Not tonight.

CHAPTER 61

ALLIE

shvale Glen stood quiet beneath the broken street sign. The others were silent beside her, but Allie felt it, the echo of the vision she and Erik once shared.

Now, only the road waited. They moved forward, boots striking wet stone. Around them, the city shifted. Old wards stirred. The house came into view three turns later.

It rose behind iron gates, half-hidden by overgrown trees. Pale stone. Shuttered windows. Victorian, with sharp lines and narrow gables. It looked like something time had forgotten.

Erik reached the gate first and unlatched it. The others followed in silence.

Elena was already waiting in the entry hall. She smiled gently, her voice smooth and pleasant.

"You made it," she said. "I hoped you would."

The hall stretched long behind her, lined in deep red wallpaper and portraits too faded to recognize. A chandelier flickered above them.

Allie hesitated. The pendant pulsed again, as if it knew this place.

Elena noticed. Her gaze tracked the pendant, then Allie's face.

"You wear it well," she said. "Serena's line never did fade."

249

Erik stiffened. "You knew? About her bloodline?"

Elena's gaze shifted to him, calm but pointed.

"Our line recognizes itself." Her smile returned, soft and sad. "Some things, Erik, are too old to hide."

Allie stepped forward, her voice firmer now.

"We came because we saw you. In the Glen. In a vision. It felt like…"

She bit back the rest. This was not the time for riddles. Not the time for ancient bloodlines and cryptic smiles. They needed answers, not mythology.

Elena's smile faltered. For just a breath, her expression cracked.

"The Glen," she said, almost to herself. Then, sharper, louder, "I don't want to talk about that."

Erik stepped closer.

"We just want to understand…"

"No." The word hit hard. She turned away, one hand braced against the hallway wall. Then the calm returned, slipping over her like a mask.

"Come," she said. "Let's find you some answers. I've a library downstairs. Old books. Older truths."

The air shifted. It grew denser, as if the house itself were listening. Still, no one moved to stop her.

Torvald muttered under his breath. Kael's jaw tightened. Still, they followed.

Elena led them down a staircase hidden behind the dining room. The wood creaked. Candles lined the descent.

The basement opened into a wide chamber. Stone floor. Chalk circles. Threads of sigils carved into the walls.

Moira stood near the center, barefoot, white-clad, smiling. Magic touched her skin.

To the left, a shape stirred. Eleanor. Bound. Head lowered. Breathing. Bruised.

Allie gasped.

She stepped forward before anyone could stop her.

CHAPTER 62

ERIK

rik lunged, slamming into Allie's shoulder before she could cross the threshold. Fire flared in his hand, ready to burn through whatever waited beyond the door.

The moment his boot hit the stone floor inside, the flame vanished. Not faded. Gone.

Cold surged in to fill the space. His scars went numb. The marks that had burned for days fell silent.

But the bond remained. Distant. Dimmed beneath the weight of the spell, but still there.

He reached for it. For her. Pushing his mind through the fog.

I'm still here.

Across the room, Allie turned her head, slow and strained. Her eyes found his.

Behind him, Torvald cursed, low, vicious. Kael staggered, one hand at her throat. The floor pulsed beneath them. Soft. Insistent.

Sigils flared to life along the walls, crawling into patterns Erik recognized too late. Containment. Suppression. A cage built for dragons.

From behind curtain seams and shadowed columns, the Watchers stepped forward. Unarmed. Unhurried. Wrapped in silence. Their eyes glowed faintly. Ancient. Empty.

The room was the weapon.

Erik tried to summon heat again. Reached for the fire that had always answered. Nothing.

At the room's entry stood Elena. Her hands were folded. Her smile, small and satisfied.

"Now that we're all here," she said, "we can begin."

Behind them, the door sealed.

Allie spun toward it. The pendant at her throat flared bright. The light struck the ward line, and died. Swallowed whole.

Erik felt the bond stutter.

Elena circled the room. Around each of them, one step at a time.

"You were always going to come," she said. "All of you. The storm. The fire. The air."

Torvald tried to step forward, fists clenched. The air shimmered around him, trying to answer. Nothing came.

Kael's knees buckled. She caught herself on the wall. "What did you do?"

Elena's smile widened. "I took away the lies you told yourselves. Your power. Your bloodlines. Your refusal to let go."

She reached the edge of the sigil circle. The five outer marks pulsed brighter.

Then the center ignited. Lines of light rose from the stone, forming a cage within the cage. Inside it stood Moira. Barefoot. Arms spread. The sixth sigil waited beneath her feet. Dark. Hungry.

Erik felt the pull again. Stronger now. Not from the bond. From the circle itself. It wanted completion. It wanted Allie.

Elena's gaze settled on her. "The sixth mark arrives."

Allie stepped back. The pendant at her throat flared again, brighter this time. But the light folded inward. Feeding the circle instead of fighting it.

Elena's smile faltered. For a heartbeat, the room held its breath. Then the circle tightened. The air folded inward.

And the real ritual began.

CHAPTER 63

MOIRA

*M*oira stood at the center, bare feet pressed to cold stone. The sigils beneath the floor thrummed in time with her heartbeat, and the house above seemed to breathe with her. It was almost ready.

The door opened. Footsteps echoed, four sets. Moira's eyes snapped open as they entered and Elena greeted them with a voice too calm to trust. They were not supposed to be here. Not yet. Not like this. Her gaze flicked to the far wall. Eleanor still bound, still bleeding. No message delivered. And still, they had come.

She let her expression smooth into calm. The storm girl stepped forward first, the pendant at her throat pulsing with defiance. "Let her go."

Moira turned slowly. Eleanor remained slumped, wrists raw from the containment thread, eyes fierce beneath the bruises. "Soon," Moira said softly, before Elena could speak. "When it's finished."

The pendant flared. Light cut across the space and slammed into Moira like a blade. Pain seared through her. Sharp. Sudden. The weave beneath her skin spasmed, and she hissed. Elena's voice drifted from outside the circle. "Careful."

But Moira only laughed, low and quiet. "She bites. Good." She reached out again. The light struck harder. The air cracked between them. For a moment, power collided. Moira staggered. Allie's eyes burned with storm-light.

"You can't take me," Allie said.

Moira's smile returned, thinner now. "You don't have the power to hurt me." But the pendant was no longer shielding. It was channeling. Feeding. The floor sigils responded, blazing to life.

Eleanor jerked against her bonds. Something gave. A thread snapped. She fell forward, free for a breath. "Allie!" she cried. The sound cracked the room like a spell.

Moira turned sharply. The older woman reached for the girl again, mouth shaping her name. Moira moved without thinking. Her hand closed, and the magic obeyed. One sharp pulse. Eleanor's chest caved. She collapsed. No sound. No breath.

For a single heartbeat, no one moved. Then Allie screamed. The storm detonated from her chest. Lightning burst from the pendant and tore across the chamber, slamming into Moira's shoulder. Flesh ripped. The pendant dimmed. Allie crumpled to her knees, spent.

Moira stepped forward, blood running down her arm. Before the others could move, she caught Allie by the throat.

From the edge of the circle, Elena's voice came steady. "Bring her to the center."

Moira obeyed. Allie's body lifted into the air, locked in place. She hovered above the sixth mark. The moment her feet touched stone, the circle surged. Sigils ignited, first in sequence, then all at once.

White fire tore through the carved lines, spiraling up the walls. The air grew thick, heavy with pressure. Kael shouted. Erik lunged. Torvald slammed both fists into the barrier. Nothing gave. Only the light did. And it was still growing.

Moira stood above her, blood still dripping freely. "It's beginning," she said.

The light answered.

CHAPTER 64

ELENA

The room spun in chaos. Power churned through the chamber like a tide. The ancient Watchers stood like sentries along the walls, their pale eyes fixed on the dragons. Every time Erik tried to summon fire, every time Kael reached for wind, the Watchers' magic tightened and forced them back.

Moira's grip on Allie was iron as she dragged her toward the center. Sigils pulsed on the floor, five of them glowing, the sixth dark but waiting. Elena moved like a shadow. She saw the confusion in Erik's desperate lunge, the shock on Allie's face, the single-minded focus in Moira's movements. And she smiled.

The knife in her hand hummed with the power of five completed marks. Moira shoved Allie into place, and the sixth sigil flickered faintly beneath her feet.

"The sixth mark is ready," Moira said. "Morna will rise through her."

Elena stepped behind her. The blade slid across Moira's throat in one fluid arc. Blood sprayed, splashing across the sixth sigil. It ignited, red light bursting upward as the circle sealed. Moira's body dropped. Elena kicked it aside without a glance.

Earth, bound in Milo. Fire, carried by Carlos. Air, shaped by

255

Marcus. Water, woven through Lena's blood. Storm, claimed by Mara. And now, spirit. Moira.

The circle was whole.

At its center, bound in rising light, stood the vessel. Allie did not move. The sigils locked her in place. Power thrummed through her veins, not her own, something ancient and vast. She could not scream. She could barely think.

Elena approached, the knife still wet in her hand. Her expression was calm. "The vessel is prepared," she said. "Take her, Mother of Grief. Rise through the storm-born. Rise."

She raised the blade. Its point hovered over Allie's heart. The chant deepened. The words that followed were old commands, spoken in a language older than mercy.

Erik lunged. Fire caught in his hand as he drew from the bond. He hit the ward line hard. Light flared. The circle resisted.

Elena's breath caught. He had drawn too much. More than he could hold. He did not understand what would happen if the bond snapped while Allie stood in the center. She remembered Jacob clawing at his chest, collapsing when the tether broke. The girl would be lost. The ritual would collapse.

Something inside her flinched. She let it pass.

Erik stumbled forward again, his fire guttering. Allie had begun to rise. Not lifted. Dragged. Light pooled beneath her feet as she left the ground.

Elena moved before thought could follow. She laughed, triumphant, certain. But Erik did not fall. The girl did not break. The tether did not snap.

Elena's grin cracked. This was wrong. The bond should have buckled by now. Why was it holding?

Then she understood.

The muting spell was not just caging their power. It was shielding the bond. Masking it. Containing it. Holding it steady before the circle could tear it apart.

She realized it moments before the lightning tore across the room, gold and jagged. The sealed windows screamed. Wind rushed in like a living force.

The curse surged upward to meet it. The circle shuddered. Power spilled through the carved lines.

And the world broke open.

Light. Sound. Blood.

And the storm claimed its own.

CHAPTER 65

ALLIE

*A*llie floated in the light. The void stretched around her, vast and pale, its silence wrapped in static. The sky above fractured and remade itself, shards of fire and storm wheeling endlessly in slow orbit. Morna stood at the center of it all. Her eyes were the pale stillness of winter. Her hair trailed frost and memory. A crown of thorns and ash circled her brow, brittle and beautiful.

"Daughter of Serena," Morna said, her voice the crack of ice across stone. "You stand beyond my curse."

Allie steadied herself. Her voice did not echo here. It simply existed, like breath inside still water. "Am I here to break the curse?"

Morna tilted her head. Her gaze, sharp as broken ice, swept across Allie like wind across a plain. "You ask questions as if you've the right."

"I don't know why I'm here. You pulled me into this. So talk to me. Show me what this is."

"You are a child of storm and fire," Morna said. "You carry the line of the one who didn't need me."

"Serena?" Allie asked. The name changed the sky. It tightened. Flinched.

Morna's mouth flattened. "She healed what I broke. She loved what I cursed."

"She found a dragon in the snow," Allie said. "She saved him."

"She defied my will," Morna whispered. "She made room for mercy in a world I buried in vengeance." Her hands moved through the air like threads. With every gesture, the void shimmered. A vision unfolded behind her: snow falling, a girl kneeling, golden light blooming from her hands.

"She didn't see the chains I'd forged. She only saw a wound and reached to mend it."

"That's not a weakness," Allie said. "That's the only reason I exist."

"Yes," Morna said quietly. "You are the echo of her mistake."

Allie's jaw clenched. "I wasn't a mistake."

A second memory bled through: flames roaring from the earth, a man's scream torn short, a woman kneeling in the mud with blood running from her eyes.

"That was Torin," Allie said softly.

"My husband," Morna answered. "My soul's match. Burned by the magic I begged to save him."

"I saw what you did," Allie said. "You cursed the dragons to make them feel what you felt."

Morna's eyes met hers. "And what did I feel?"

"Loss," Allie said. "You lost everything."

"And now you understand. You've lost parents. Sister. Friend. And if that woman is kin to you, more loss still. And soon the fire-born will be gone as well." Morna's voice deepened. "You think me cruel, but I only mirrored what the world gave me."

The silence between them pulsed.

"I didn't ask to inherit this. You cursed the dragons. And you made the Watchers keep it alive."

"I made sure the wound stayed visible."

"And what now?" Allie asked. "You want me to finish what you started?"

Morna looked at her for a long time. "No," she said at last. "Would you choose differently."

"I don't even know what the choice is." Allie's heart pounded. The pendant at her throat flickered, gold sparks dancing in rhythm with her breath.

"You said magic answers need," Allie whispered.

Morna nodded once. Her voice softened, almost gentle. "Then choose. The vessel is prepared. The pattern is complete. Let me in, and I will carry it forward. I will burn what must be burned. I will return."

Allie blinked. "Return? You want to come back?"

"Let me in," Morna said, "and I will rise through you. I've waited millennia for the pattern to be fulfilled. You are the vessel. You were always meant to be."

"And you believe I'll just... let you?"

The void tightened. The storm above groaned. Morna stepped closer, hand outstretched. "I will burn the dragons. I will bring magic back. I will make them suffer as they made me suffer. Choose. If you don't, it will be made for you, and you won't survive."

The sigils stirred beneath the void, faint echoes carved in light. Each one a wound, a tether, a name spoken in pain. Storm bore the weight of memory. The spirit held the thread. Together, they did not just mark. They remembered. Not stone, not blood, but will. Each line drawn in sacrifice. Each spiral a map of grief turned ritual. And in the final mark, the curse waited, not to be spoken, but to be answered.

Her form shifted. Shadows spread from her feet. The frost in her hair curled like smoke. Her crown darkened. Her eyes went hollow. The void changed with her, sharp and jagged, the air charged with unseen teeth.

Allie trembled. Storm-light surged behind her ribs. Her hand rose, light blooming along her fingers.

"No."

Morna flinched. "What are you doing?"

"I said no."

Light flared from her palm. The pendant blazed gold, brighter than anything else in the void. The sky cracked above, splitting down the middle like torn silk.

Morna's expression twisted in rage. "You can't hold me back. The circle is complete."

"But the choice is mine." Allie's voice deepened. It filled the void. Her arm shook with power. Storm-light spilled from her mouth, from her hands, from her chest.

The void howled. The air itself tried to close.

And then... a warmth beside her. A pull in her chest. She turned.

Erik stood beside her, his hand closing around hers.

The others had failed because they broke the bond.

She had kept it.

Together, they were the key.

Fire and storm met without fear.

The void pulsed.

The sky breathed.

CHAPTER 66

ERIK

*E*rik lunged. His hand lit with fire. The ward line flared. He hit it hard.

The curse surged to meet Allie. The circle shuddered. Power flooded the lines.

The world fractured.

Light. Sound. Blood.

And the storm claimed its own.

The force struck like a tidal wave. Elena flew from the circle, slammed into the far wall. Her knife clattered away.

The Watchers hurled like rags against stone.

Erik's barrier dissolved. He staggered forward, the bond yanking him toward the center.

Allie hovered, suspended. Frozen. Light poured from her. Sigils pulsed beneath her.

"Allie!"

He ran. Boots cracked stone. The room groaned.

He reached her. Grasped her hand.

The world shifted.

Everything fell away.

He stood on cold stone. Wind howled in a void of storm and shadow. Her hand remained in his, warm and real.

Allie stood beside him, hair lifting, storm-light in her eyes.

Before them loomed Morna.

No longer a woman. Sorrow given shape. Towering, wrapped in ash and frost. Her eyes burned with grief.

Allie's hand tightened. "Erik? How are you…"

"The bond," he said, pulling her close. "It pulled me in."

Morna's gaze sharpened. "All others failed. Storm alone could never break my curse. But fire and storm together…"

She stepped forward. Her hand reached toward Erik, white with frostbite. Cold needled his skin, threading into the heat beneath his ribs.

His fire fought, then faltered.

A line appeared.

Not light. Not flame. A chain.

Silver and sharp, forged from sorrow. Linking her to him, loop after loop etched with dragon sigils.

The air filled with its sound.

Morna's voice broke the silence. "You are mine, fire-born. You all are. Your flame is the debt I bound to grief."

Erik's knees buckled. Cold crawled up his throat. He felt them, the others, echoes of lost dragons, hearts beating inside the chain.

Allie's voice cut through the wind. "What is that?"

Silver burned brighter. Links tightened, pulling Morna and Erik closer. His fire flared red against white.

Allie stepped forward. Her hand rose to reach between Morna and Erik.

Morna's eyes widened. "No."

Allie's fingers brushed the light.

The world convulsed.

The chain screamed. Links turned molten, gold bleeding through silver. Every mark lit in sequence.

Links cracked. One. Then another.

Morna cried out, frost pouring from her mouth.

The chain tore in a blaze of color, fragments dissolving.

Erik's fire roared free, bright and terrible.

Morna staggered, clutching emptiness. Her eyes were wide and hollow.

The curse broke.

And the world knew.

A sound rolled through. Grief unchained.

Erik dropped to one knee. Breath tore through his lungs. Fire surged wild. For a heartbeat, he thought he might break apart.

But he did not.

He clenched his jaw. Grounded himself in his magic. In the bond with Allie.

She is here. She is real. Move.

Torvald grunted nearby, his fist against the wall as golden light cracked through stone.

Kael dropped to one knee, her wind-stone shattering.

The Watchers screamed.

Bodies convulsed as false power turned inward. Marks sizzled off skin. Some ran. Others collapsed, whispering to a goddess who was no longer listening.

The floor pulsed. The air trembled.

Morna screamed again, not in pain but in fury.

She flung magic at Allie.

Erik moved before thought.

He stepped in front of the strike. Took the hit meant for her.

It slammed into his chest, driving breath from his lungs. Pain lanced through him.

His hand tore free of hers.

The realm rejected him.

He flew into the void.

The last thing he saw was Morna turning toward Allie, fury redoubling.

Then a voice.

One eye fluttered open. Torvald was there, pale and bleeding, his hand on Erik's shoulder.

"Erik," he said.

Then everything turned black.

CHAPTER 67

ALLIE

*E*rik's hand tore from hers. The bond snapped. Allie stumbled forward, breath catching.

No.

He was gone. Vanished into the dark.

Her fingers curled into fists.

"You took him," she shouted. "You took him like you took everything else."

Morna stood tall, frost flaring from her eyes. "He was fire. Fire always burns."

Allie's breath hitched. Power gathered low in her chest. The pendant at her throat burned bright.

"I won't let you do this," she said. "I'll finish what Elena started."

"You'll do nothing."

Morna raised her hand, and the void twisted. Ice snaked around Allie's limbs, rooting her in place. The cold climbed her arms, her legs, her throat. It dug into her collarbone and drew blood.

"I'm still the architect of this place," Morna hissed. "And I haven't yet decided what to do with you."

She stepped closer.

"You think mercy will save you. But I've known no mercy."

267

Allie choked on the cold. "I feel sorry for you, then. Just end it."

Morna's eyes narrowed. Her hand lifted again.

A voice cut through the void.

"Morna."

Soft. Male. Familiar.

Allie's breath caught. Her magic wavered.

Morna turned.

Torin stood just beyond the reach of the light. Whole. Young. Holding the child in his arms.

His gaze held only sorrow. And gentleness.

"We've been waiting," he said.

Morna's hand fell to her side. Her crown cracked, frost crumbling down her cheeks.

She stepped forward.

"I lost you," she said.

"You didn't," he whispered. "We've been right here. Waiting."

The baby gurgled softly.

Morna's form flickered. The storm inside her stilled.

"Come home, my love," Torin said.

She reached for them.

As her fingers brushed the child's skin, the void filled with gold.

Not fire. Not frost. Forgiveness.

The storm broke. The light unraveled.

And Morna was gone.

The void collapsed. The sky mended.

Allie fell.

She struck cracked stone, knees slamming down, palms scraping across scorched sigils. The circle was broken. The air hung heavy, thick with smoke.

It was over.

She pushed herself upright, breath sharp and fast. The chamber still trembled faintly. Faint sigils glowed in the cracks.

Her gaze caught on movement.

Torvald knelt beside Erik near the edge of the circle, one hand pressed to the wound at his side. Erik's fire had guttered out.

"Come on," Torvald muttered. "You've clawed your way out of worse."

Erik stirred, a sound breaking loose from his throat. His eyes fluttered open. Barely.

Allie stumbled toward them. The bond had broken in the void. But now, as her hand touched his again, something fragile stirred beneath the surface. Not whole. But still there.

"Erik."

He turned his head, just enough to find her. His lips moved. No words. Just her name.

She took his hand. It was warm, even now. It was enough.

Across the room, Kael's storm-light still flickered. She had Elena pinned to the far wall, her hand raised.

Elena's eyes burned wild. Rage flickered in them.

"She lied to me," Elena spat. "She said she'd restore me. That Morna would give me back what she took."

Kael didn't answer.

Elena's laugh cracked like breaking bone. "I did everything. Every mark. Every life. And for what? Another failure."

Her power bled away, leaving only smoke.

Allie turned.

Eleanor's body lay near the base of the stairs, her hand outstretched. The sight hollowed something inside Allie.

She knelt beside her aunt. Her voice was a whisper.

"I'm sorry."

No answer came.

Moira's body lay crumpled near the edge of the circle, pale and still, eyes open but empty.

Allie rose again, her chest tight.

The Watchers that remained lingered at the edges, whispering among themselves. Some were burned, some half-mad. When Allie's gaze met theirs, they looked away. Then, one by one, they began to retreat, slipping through broken doorways like smoke.

Allie turned back to Erik. He was still breathing. Barely.

Kael joined them, her storm-stone cracked and dim. She crouched beside Torvald and touched Erik's shoulder.

The four of them sat in the silence of what remained.

The air felt different now. Lighter.

Torvald looked up first. "It's gone. I can feel it. The curse is gone."

Allie looked at Erik's hand in hers. The chain that had bound the dragons for a thousand years was broken.

But the cost filled the room.

"Yes," she whispered. "It's gone."

Her gaze swept the ruined chamber one last time.

Outside, thunder rolled. Distant. Final.

And the storm began to clear.

EPILOGUE

A FEW DAYS LATER

The city was quieter than it should have been.

Allie leaned against the rusted railing of the hospital rooftop, watching the last edge of the sun sink behind the skyline. From here, Dallas looked almost peaceful. The chaos that had gripped it, sigils blazing and sky cracked with lightning, felt distant now.

But the bond at her throat still thrummed. The scar on her palm itched. And every time she closed her eyes, she saw threads. Golden. Fraying. Cut.

"You're not supposed to be up here."

Kael's voice drifted from the stairwell door. She stepped into the light, hands shoved into her coat pockets.

Allie shrugged. "Sue me."

Kael came to stand beside her. For a moment, they just watched the city together.

"How's Erik?" Kael asked quietly.

"Stubborn. Healing. Alive." Allie glanced down at the bond. "Barely got him into the hospital. They said his vitals kept shifting. Like the machines couldn't read him."

"Storm-born. Untethered now. They'll need to recalibrate everything."

271

"I keep thinking, if I'd been faster..."

"You were fast enough." Kael's tone cut through the guilt. "You broke the curse. Saved Erik. Saved a city full of dragons who didn't know they were bleeding to death. You did everything."

Allie looked down at her hands. "I didn't mean to. I just... reacted."

"That's how real magic works."

They stood in silence for a while longer.

Then Kael said, "The Alliance sent word."

Allie raised an eyebrow. "What, they want to thank me?"

"They want to watch you." Kael's jaw tightened. "A storm-bonded human who severed a thousand-year curse? You scare the hell out of them."

"Good."

A ghost of a smile crossed Kael's face. "I told them if they tried anything, I'd burn down their archives."

"You really are a terrible dragon."

"I try."

Allie pulled the matchbook from her coat pocket. It was weather-worn now, ink fading at the corners.

Dragon's Breath. Midnight.

"You think William'll be okay?" she asked.

Kael hesitated. "Torvald's people found him. He's going under-ground for now. He's older than we know. Stronger than we thought. And hurting. He asked not to be found. Old dragons need time and space for healing."

"Will he be back?"

Kael looked at her. "One day."

They let that sit. Shadows cooling into night.

"How's Elena?" Allie asked softly.

"In custody. The Alliance won't touch her. Too public. Too messy. She confessed to everything, but..." Kael paused. "She's broken. She's not beyond repair."

Allie did not argue.

Instead, she looked back toward the city. Lights flickered on.

"Everything's different now, isn't it?" she whispered.

"Yeah."

"And it's not over."

"No." Kael leaned on the railing. "But you don't have to face it alone."

Allie turned her head. Their eyes met.

"You know," she said, "I'm not a Watcher. I'm not a dragon. I'm not anything."

Kael's smile was tired. And real. "That's not exactly true. Just because we don't know what you are yet doesn't mean you're nothing."

She shrugged, that old spark of humor returning. "You could be a dragon. You could be a mega dragon. Or a mega witch. Or just a little witch with attitude."

Allie snorted.

Kael nudged her shoulder. "We'll figure it out. Takes time, little grasshopper."

Allie rolled her eyes.

The wind lifted. For a moment, it smelled like ozone and fire. Then just rain.

The wind shifted again. Not hard. Not loud. Just... strange.

Allie straightened. Her gaze moved toward the north, to the place where the ritual site had burned.

"What is it?" Kael asked.

"I don't know," Allie whispered.

The sky was breaking open.

From the far edge of the city, a shimmer lit the clouds. Not lightning. Not fire. Something else.

A hum reached them, low, steady.

Then they heard the sound of wings.

First one figure emerged from the haze. Then another. Side by side.

Not as ghosts. Not as shadows. As light.

Mara appeared first, her outline flickering, her form more soul than skin. Her eyes, when they found the rooftop, found Allie and then Kael, were full of something vast. No pain. No fear. Only love.

And Lena, larger, quieter, glowed like moonlight beside her. Her face turned to Allie, and even from this distance, Allie felt it. That invisible thread between them tugging once, twice, then letting go.

The spirits stepped forward together. And then they changed.

Not violently. Not with pain. With purpose.

Light burst from their chests. Their shapes stretched, lifted, transformed. Hair became flame. Arms became wings. Skin gave way to scale.

Two dragons rose into the sky.

Mara, small and brilliant, silver and blue.

Lena, vast but no less radiant, all white fire and grace.

Allie's breath caught. The bond at her throat thrummed in recognition, a final farewell.

Beside her, Kael pressed a hand to her heart, where she wore Mara's old medallion Allie had given her for graduation.

"They're whole," she said.

The dragons circled once above the city. They did not roar. They did not cry. But the world felt it.

Then, together, they lifted. Up. Into cloud. Into wind. Into whatever came next.

And they were gone.

Allie stood rooted. Her fingers curled tight around the railing. Her eyes burned.

"Did that really happen?" she asked.

Kael did not answer at first. Then she said, very softly, "Yeah."

Silence stretched. But it did not feel empty.

Allie's voice trembled. "You think we'll see them again?"

Kael turned her face to the sky with a small smile. "We can in dreams."

Kael's phone buzzed. She glanced at it, then looked up at Allie.

"Reports coming in. Dragons all over the city, all over the world, they can feel it. The curse's weight is gone." She paused. "Freed but still earthbound."

"So what does that mean?" Allie asked.

"It means," Kael said carefully, "you broke the curse. You freed us all. But that didn't restore us. Not completely."

The two of them looked out over the city. Somewhere, living dragons were waking to their freedom, even if they could not yet spread their wings. Somewhere, the old order was crumbling.

"So we're free," Allie said slowly. "But not fixed."

"Free's enough for now," Kael said. "We'll figure out the rest as we go."

Somewhere, the world was changing.

And they had no idea what came next.

Kael pulled the medallion from beneath her shirt. Mara's medallion. The metal was warm, like it had caught fire from the transformation.

For a moment, she could have sworn she heard a voice on the wind. Not words. Just music. A saxophone riff, bright and wild and free.

She smiled through her tears.

"Yeah," she whispered to the sky. "I hear you."

Allie's hand found hers. They stood together, two women who had loved the same impossible girl, watching the place where dragons had flown.

"Thank you," Allie said quietly. "For protecting me. For believing me."

"Thank Mara," Kael said. "She taught me what's worth fighting for."

The wind rose, gentle this time, like an answer.

"We should get back," Allie said. "Check on Erik."

"Yeah, I need to see what the Alliance is planning. And maybe sleep for a week," Kael added.

"That too."

They turned from the railing, leaving the empty sky behind.

Tomorrow would bring new questions. New challenges. A world that did not know what it was becoming.

But tonight, they had won. And for now, that was enough.

* * *

HOSPITAL ROOM

The machines had stopped beeping.

Erik's vitals were stable now, though the nurses still came in every few hours pretending not to stare at the bond mark across his chest. They could not explain the fluctuations. Could not explain how his body ran warm enough to melt thermometers and still showed no fever.

They just called it trauma. Allie knew better.

She sat beside him in the dark, curled in the corner chair with her knees pulled to her chest and Eleanor's book on her lap. She had not opened it yet.

The last time she had, nothing had happened.

"You're watching me breathe again."

Erik's voice was gravel and smoke.

Allie looked up. "You stopped breathing for a minute. That gives me a pass for at least another day."

He shifted in the bed and winced. "If I tell you I'm fine, will you sleep?"

"No."

A ghost of a smile touched his face. He looked older now. Tired. But something in him had eased, like a spring finally uncoiled.

"How's Kael?" he asked.

"Still trying to convince the Alliance not to mark me as a threat."

"Good luck with that."

"You're not helping."

"I almost died."

"You did die. For like fifteen seconds."

"All the more reason you should be nice to me," he said.

She raised a brow. "How long are you planning to milk that cow?"

He smirked, eyes half-lidded. "Give or take another century."

Allie blinked. "Wait. *Another*? Seriously?"

"I lost track around the Cold War. Time gets weird when you're trying not to be noticed."

Her mouth dropped open. "Are you telling me I'm bonded with a guy who's old enough to remember rotary phones?"

"I remember telegram codes," he said, smug.

She groaned and dragged a hand down her face. "Oh my God. I kissed my grandpa!"

"You never asked."

"Next time I'm checking IDs."

"You wouldn't believe mine if I showed you."

She snorted. "You were unconscious for two days. This is how you come back?"

He opened one eye. "Did I ask for a whiskey yet?"

"Not until you can stand."

He looked at her then, really looked. "You cut the curse, Allie."

"I didn't mean to."

"That doesn't matter."

She traced the edge of the book with one finger. "It felt like... threads. All of it. And one was silver. And I just..."

"You saw it. No one else could've."

"Why me?"

Silence again. Allie let out a breath.

"In the last four days, I've seen things I didn't think were real, things I still don't have words for. I've watched magic rise, storms split open the sky. I've felt power that could end cities."

She paused, voice softer.

"I saw two people I loved, who were gone, become something I thought only existed in stories. Dragons, Erik. Not monsters. Not metaphors. Beautiful. Free."

Her throat tightened. "It's almost too much to hold. And yet... it's mine to carry."

Rain tapped the window. Somewhere down the hall, a nurse laughed.

Erik shifted again, slower this time. "Do you regret it?"

"No." She said it without hesitation. "But I'm scared."

"Good," he said, voice low. "That means you're sane."

"I saw too much."

"So did I."

He shifted carefully, ignoring the pull of the IVs, propping himself onto one elbow.

"The curse is broken, but the damage isn't undone. Others like me. Bound for too long. They won't know what to do with their freedom."

"I don't know what to do with mine."

"You'll learn."

She met his eyes. Storm and fire.

"I think I need to read this book."

He nodded. "And when you do... maybe you'll write the next one."

Allie closed her hand over the cover. "Not yet."

She stood and crossed to the bed, sitting at the edge.

"You scared me," she said quietly.

"You scare me every time you look at me like that."

He blinked. "Like what?"

"Like you see the good."

His voice dropped, low and steady. "Because it's there."

He reached up and took her hand. She let him.

"I'm glad it was you," he said.

"So am I."

They sat like that, hands twined, hearts syncing. The bond shimmered at the edges, not broken, not tamed, just them. Wild and real and still standing.

He tugged her hand gently. Just a small pull. Not a demand, just a request for closeness.

She pulled back. Crossed to the far corner of the room with a sharp look over her shoulder.

"I told you no."

His mouth curved, slow and dangerous. "You remember what I said about that word?"

"I remember," she said. Arms crossed. Unmoving.

"I'm working with limited resources," he added, gesturing faintly to the bed, the wires, the bruises. "If I weren't stuck in this thing..."

She narrowed her eyes. The air between them went tight, bright.

He crooked a finger. "Come here."

She gave him the finger instead.

He laughed, head tipping back, shoulders easing into the pillow.

Then he leaned in slightly, voice low, thick with amusement. "I'm not above making you say it twice."

She arched a brow. "I'm not above shocking a dragon into silence."

"I dare you."

She stopped, just for a beat. Her eyes narrowed slightly.

"I stopped Morna with one word," she said.

He blinked. His mouth fell open. "You stopped the ancient, dragon-ending curse-witch... with *no*?"

The word hung between them.

Allie's smile turned razor-sharp, slow and deliberate. She leaned in, close enough that her breath brushed his ear, voice dropping to a purr.

"It worked wonders on her," she whispered. "Wonder how it'll work on you."

He reached for her, fingers snagging the hem of her shirt, tugging her closer with a growl, the bond sparking static between them.

She pulled back just far enough to watch his reaction, eyes glittering with challenge.

Then she started forward, slow, deliberate. The corner of her mouth lifted.

"You asking nicely?"

He crooked the same finger. "Not even a little."

She came to a stop at the edge of the bed. Her gaze dipped, then returned to his with heat.

She let the silence stretch, long enough for heat to coil low in her stomach.

Long enough for him to notice.

"So," she said, almost thoughtful. "This is the part where I finally find out what a dragon looks like naked?"

To be continued...

AUTHOR'S NOTE

Thank you for reading Fire & Light!

This book has been a labor of love, grief, and magic. If you enjoyed Allie and Erik's story, please consider leaving a review on Amazon or Goodreads. Reviews help readers discover new books, and I read every single one.

The Dragonfire saga continues in Earth & Shadow, coming Fall 2026.

Want to be the first to know when it releases?

Join my newsletter at www.lovelight-books.com.

Dragons, storms, and Dallas await.

Until next time,

Lovelight

ACKNOWLEDGMENTS

First and foremost, thank you to Sam, my daughter, and Todd, my friend for believing in this story even when I didn't.

To my beta readers, your feedback made this book infinitely better.

Thank you for your honesty, enthusiasm, and patience with my many questions about dragon logistics.

To my design team, who brought Fire & Light to life in ways I couldn't have imagined.

To my family, thank you for the encouragement, the commiseration, and the late-night brainstorming sessions.

To the readers who take a chance on debut authors, thank you. You're the reason books like this get to exist in the world.

And finally, to anyone who's ever felt like the storm inside them was too big to hold: You're not alone. Let it out. The world needs your lightning.

ABOUT THE AUTHOR

Lovelight writes urban fantasy and paranormal romance from Wichita Falls, Texas.

When not writing about dragons and magic, she can be found selling real estate, drinking too much coffee and plotting the next book in the series.

Fire & Light is her debut novel.

Connect online:
Website: www.lovelight-books.com
Newsletter: www.lovelight-books.com

[O] instagram.com/lovelight_writer
[J] tiktok.com/@lovelight_writer
[f] facebook.com/lovelight
[P] patreon.com/Lovelight_books

EARTH & SHADOW

DRAGONFIRE SAGA - BOOK TWO

BY LOVELIGHT

Allie's apartment smelled like burned toast.

She emerged from the bedroom with damp hair and a towel looped around her neck, following the scent like a warning. Erik stood at the stove with a spatula in one hand and a look of intense concentration, as if he were defusing a bomb instead of cooking breakfast.

The pan in front of him hissed ominously.

"You're a dragon," Allie said. "Literal fire magic. How are you this bad at cooking?"

"Fire magic burns things," he said without looking up. "Cooking requires not burning things. The skills are opposed."

She stepped closer and peered into the pan. "That's definitely burned."

"It's... caramelized."

"It's carbon."

He sighed and turned off the burner. "Coffee?"

"Please."

They had been living together for six weeks now. Temporarily. Just until Erik healed. Just until the city stopped shaking from what they had done. Just until someone came up with a better plan.

No one had.

Neither of them had suggested he leave.

Allie moved past him and reached for the mugs. The kitchen window over the sink looked out onto the street four floors below. From here she could see the single old tree clinging to life near the curb, its trunk split and scarred where some car had clipped it years ago. A faded orange tag hung from one low branch, the city's way of promising to remove it and never quite following through.

It should have been dead already.

It was not.

She tried not to think about that.

She filled the mugs while Erik scraped the ruined eggs into the trash. Morning light slanting across the counter caught the pale threads of the bond mark at her collarbone. She had stopped trying to hide it. Someone always noticed it anyway when she wore anything that dipped too low. Semicircles of silver and gold braided together where Morna's curse had once tried to tear them apart.

The mark hummed quietly beneath her skin. It was not the sharp crackle of storm she had come to expect. It was deeper than that. Slower. Almost like a second heartbeat under the first, as if something in the earth itself had started breathing again and forgotten how to stop.

She told herself it was in her head.

"Don't look at me like that," Erik said.

She passed him a mug. "Like what."

"Like you're about to file charges on my breakfast."

"It left evidence," she said. "There are crumbs and everything."

The corner of his mouth tugged up. He looked older some days, shadows etched deeper at the edges of his eyes, but there was something looser in his posture now. Less of the constant braced-for-impact tension he had carried when the curse still sat on his shoulders like a second spine.

"Come on," he said. "Balcony. Before the smoke alarm adds its opinion."

They stepped out onto the narrow balcony that overlooked the street. The city rose around them in glass and steel, morning light already catching on windows and distant cranes. Somewhere below, a bus hissed to a stop. A jogger's footsteps tapped out a steady rhythm on the sidewalk.

The old tree near the curb stood just within her view, its branches thin and bare of anything but a few stubborn leaves. Its roots had cracked the concrete in a jagged circle, as if the earth were trying to push itself back through the street and did not care what the city wanted.

"Kael called," Erik said, leaning against the railing.

"That's ominous." Allie took a careful sip. "You lead with that before or after bad news these days."

"Before. Sometimes during." He watched steam curl from his mug. "She wants to meet at the Black Cat tonight."

Allie's fingers tightened around the ceramic. "It's reopening already."

"Under new management," Erik said. "One of the remaining dragons bought it. Kael says he wants to turn it into a community space for supernatural beings. Her words."

"Of course she found a way to turn a bar into a political statement."

"She calls it outreach."

Allie let out a breath that was almost a laugh. The idea of walking back into that alley made her stomach clench, but the thought of someone giving it a different story felt right. Maybe even necessary.

"Is William going to be there?" she asked.

"Probably not," Erik said. "He's still… adjusting."

That was one word for it.

"How is he?" she asked softly.

"He lost a century of lies in a night," Erik said. "The curse stripped away all the excuses he'd used to survive. Now he has nothing between himself and the guilt but time. He's having trouble controlling the shifts. Keeps transforming when he gets emotional."

Allie's mouth twitched. "Emotional how. Angry? Sad? Existential crisis over breakfast pastries?"

"Yesterday he was moved by a sandwich," Erik said. "Nearly became a dragon near a Subway. Torvald had to handle the cleanup."

The image of Torvald, grim and precise, dealing with a dragon incident next to a fast food sign broke through the heaviness in her chest. Allie laughed, a startled sound that felt almost normal.

"So that's a yes on emotional sandwiches," she said.

"Yes." Erik smiled into his coffee.

The pendant at her throat thrummed once, then settled. For a heartbeat, beneath the usual stormlight, she thought she felt something else. Stone. Roots. A slow, patient awareness brushing the edge of her senses. A steady pull from deep in the earth, as if something far below were trying to reach her but did not yet know her name.

She looked down at the street again. The old tree stood where it always did. Cracked. Silent. Waiting for the city to remember its promise to cut it down.

Nothing moved.

"Kael says most of the dragons still can't shift," Erik said. His tone had turned thoughtful, the way it did when he slipped into the part of himself that had once been the Alliance's blade. "They can feel the curse is gone. The weight is off. But the change won't answer when they call it."

"Like something's still holding them," Allie said.

"Yes. But it isn't Morna any longer."

"And the Watchers," Allie said quietly.

Erik nodded once. "They're adrift. Without the curse, they've no task to anchor them. Some vanished. Some cling to old habits out of fear. They look like an order waiting for a purpose that no longer exists."

She thought of the sigils burned into stone. The roar of the void. The way Morna's crown had cracked when Torin stepped from the dark with their child in his arms. The moment the world had shuddered and broken and tried to put itself back together in a new shape.

She had not meant to cut the curse. She had simply reached for the one thread that felt wrong and pulled.

"You think that's my fault too," she asked quietly.

"No." Erik's answer was immediate. "The curse is gone because you were brave enough to touch it. Whatever remains is something older. Or something left behind."

"That's very comforting," she said dryly.

"You're welcome."

They stood in silence for a moment. Wind slid around the building, cool against her face. It carried a faint scent of rain, car exhaust, and something else she could not name. Something like wet stone after a drought.

Her phone buzzed in her pocket. A news alert flashed across the screen.

MYSTERIOUS CREATURE SIGHTED OVER WHITE ROCK LAKE

A blurry photo accompanied it, all grain and motion. A shape in the clouds that could have been a trick of the light or could have been a dragon who had miscalculated the line between caution and freedom.

Allie held the phone out. "Subtle," she said.

Erik glanced at it and huffed a breath that was almost a laugh. "Someone's becoming careless."

"Or brave," Allie said.

"Perhaps both."

She lowered the phone but did not put it away. The world looked the same as it had six weeks ago. Same skyline. Same traffic. Same dented tree. Somewhere, though, everything had changed.

"What about the Alliance," she asked. "How are they handling the fact that dragons are no longer quietly dying under their watch?"

"Fragmenting," Erik said. "Some factions want to build something new. Something less secret and less cruel. Others want the old control back and pretend nothing's changed. A few are trying to walk away before anyone asks what they knew."

"So the usual chaos," she said.

"Essentially."

A breeze lifted the edge of her hair. The mark at her collarbone warmed again. The new undertone answered, a slow, steady drumbeat under the pulse of storm and fire.

There it is again, she thought.

"Have you decided about the job?" Erik asked.

She blinked and pulled herself back from the feeling. "The nonprofit."

"Yes."

The offer sat on the counter under the salt shaker, three pages of dense text and a bright logo that still made her laugh when she looked at it. Legal Advocacy for Supernatural Communities. Someone had underlined the title three times in red pen, as if to convince themselves it was real.

"They want me to head it," Allie said. "First client is a dragon who needs citizenship papers. The government doesn't seem to have a form for people who technically died three hundred years ago and then came back with a new legal name and a fire problem."

"Creative law," Erik said. "You'd be good at it."

She studied the city. "Do you think it's wise? Working in this world. Your world."

"It's your world now," he said.

"Is it?"

He turned his head to look at her fully. "Do you want it to be?"

She did not answer immediately. She thought of Kael threatening to burn down the Alliance archives if anyone touched Allie without her permission. She thought of William's tremor when he had asked not to be found for a while. She thought of Mara and Lena rising in light and wing from the hospital roof, together and finally free.

She thought of two pendants in her hand and a city that had never slept easy under fire.

"Yes," she said at last. "I think I do."

"Then it's wise," Erik said simply.

Her phone buzzed again. This time it wasn't a news alert. A message preview flashed on the screen.

William: Found something. Need you and Erik
at the workshop. Bring Eleanor's book.
Important.

Allie felt the words land like a weight in her chest. The book still sat on her nightstand, its leather cover worn soft where her thumb had traced the edges without opening it. The last time she had tried, nothing had happened.

"William," she said.

Erik's gaze sharpened. "What does he want?"

She held the phone out. He read the message once, then again, as if the meaning would change the second time.

"He says it's about the transformations," Erik said quietly. "About why most of them still can't shift."

"And he wants Eleanor's book," Allie said.

The bond mark thrummed in answer.

Erik finished his coffee in a swallow and set the mug on the balcony rail. "We should go."

"Now?"

"Yes."

Allie looked once more at the old tree by the curb. For the first time, she thought she heard something in the rustle of its thin branches. Not wind. Not traffic. A faint, strained groan, as if the trunk were trying to straighten after too many years of leaning.

She told herself it was her imagination. The world under her feet had shifted. Of course she was jumping at shadows and creaking wood.

"Come on, storm girl," Erik said. His voice was light, but his eyes were not. "Let's see what William found before he sets another restaurant on fire."

"Once," Allie said as she stepped back inside. "He set one restaurant on fire one time."

"That we know about," Erik said.

She grabbed her keys, her jacket, and Eleanor's book from the nightstand. The leather felt cooler than she remembered. Heavier. As if someone had slipped new pages into it while she slept.

They left the apartment together and headed down the stairwell. On the street, the air felt thicker, closer to the ground. Her mark pulsed once in time with the distant thud of something she could not identify.

They passed the old tree on the way to the car. Allie did not look up, but for a moment the hairs on her arms rose, as if something had turned toward her and struggled to remember the shape of a greeting.

She opened the passenger door and slid inside, telling herself it was nothing.

By the time Erik pulled away from the curb, the tree had gone still again. Its cracked branches reached toward the pale morning sky as if they were waiting for something. Or someone.

Neither of them saw the small shower of dry twigs that fell from its lowest limb as the car turned the corner and vanished from sight.

BONUS

LOVED THIS BOOK?

Reviews help readers discover new books!

If you enjoyed Fire & Light, please consider leaving a review on:
- Amazon
- Goodreads
- BookBub

Even a sentence or two makes a huge difference. Thank you for supporting indie authors!

BOOK CLUB DISCUSSION QUESTIONS

1. Allie struggles with accepting her power throughout the story. Have you ever felt afraid of your own potential? How did you overcome it?

2. Morna's grief turns to vengeance, while Serena's becomes healing. What do you think makes the difference?

3. The bond between Allie and Erik forms instantly but develops over time. Do you believe in "fated" connections, or do relationships require choice?

4. How does the Dallas setting enhance the story? Could this story happen anywhere else?

5. If you could have one character's magical ability, whose would you choose and why?